VOW TO ADORE

A FLYING CROSS RANCH ROMANCE 3

SHANAE JOHNSON

THOSE JOHNSON GIRLS

CHAPTER ONE

The chime let off a high-pitched shrill, breaking up the sounds of the music coming from the stage. A few listeners turned to glare at Will Matthews. He shrank down in his seat a bit, hating the momentary spotlight on him.

In fact, Will detested any added attention on him. Luckily, he was the third eldest in a family of six brothers -right smack-dab in the middle of the family, making it easy for him to hide. With two older and three younger loud, rambunctious, opinionated and sometimes quick-tempered boys, Will had no problems hanging out at the back of the line. Or better yet, off to the sides while his siblings shouted their imminent approach, drew attention to their presence, and were often asked to leave as a result of all of it.

Will did not like to be a bother or cause a ruckus. People would've called him quiet, except he was always flanked by at least one of his noisy brothers, who would quickly shoo away any notion of quiet. Though he sat at the table alone, it was one of his brothers calling him on his cell.

Truth be told, his ringing phone during the current stage performance was not the true ruckus being caused. It was the sad excuse for music that was bothersome. The drummer was a beat behind the keyboardist. The guitarist's E-string was out of tune. The vocalist had mixed up the words of the popular song that the whole band was butchering.

Will was sure his ringing phone couldn't possibly make the cacophony of sounds any worse. Still, he silenced the device. Though he knew that wouldn't stop the person on the other end of the phone from reaching out to him again.

He was right.

Barely a second later and the phone vibrated once more on the small, round and quite unsturdy dining table. The light from the face of the phone flashed an alert in case the bumping and jumping around of the device wasn't notification enough.

Again, the guests at the wobbly table next to him sent him a glare.

Will could've glared right back. Or he could've straightened his shoulders and puffed out his chest. He had a good fifty pounds on his glaring adversaries -combined. But confrontation was not his way. Something his family of active duty Air Force and vets had often used against him. Being the sole Matthews boy who was a pacifist, Will took it all in stride. Except the one time Will had stood his ground without backing down.

On that day, Will had stood tall, with his chest puffed up while he disappointed the man who meant the most to him in this world. When Will had broken the news to his adoptive father that had broken the old man's heart, Will hadn't blinked. Haran Matthews had taught him better than that. But Will's mind had been made up that day, and though he knew his father would never be as proud of him as he was of his other sons, Will had done what was best for himself.

And now he was going to have to do it again. But he could do it later rather than sooner. Which was the excuse he gave as to why he was now in a dive bar, listening to the butchering of old songs made into something unrecognizable by today's rebel youth. The last act had taken an old Beatles song and made it sound like frogs croaking to their death. The current act was thankfully finishing up a poor man's rendition of an Ella Fitzgerald song that made Will certain he was dreaming a little nightmare.

As that band cleared off, Will's phone took another opportunity to vibrate and flash once more. He knew this would continue until he answered. Now that Joe was out of the military, his brother would dog him until Will answered.

"Shouldn't you be in court or something?" was Will's greeting to his older brother.

"No, because I'll be headed to church instead."

"Not surprising being the kid of a preacher."

"She said *yes*."

Will paused to stare down at his phone. On the face of the receiver was his brother's name and number. Instead of the picture of his brown-skinned brother, there was the image of a woman with honey-golden skin. Her wide eyes were looking dreamily off into space. Foxy James was the woman of Joe's dreams, but Joe had never told the woman that all these years. It looked like that had just changed.

"You finally told Foxy how you feel?"

"I did."

"And now you're going to the church because... you're getting married?"

"We are."

"Bro!" Will fist pumped the air, his excitement too great to be contained. "That's the best news I've heard in a long time."

Will was truly happy for Joe. He was the most serious brother of the Matthews clan, but he'd been head over heels in love with Foxy James for as long as Will could remember. Their brother Charlie had been in love with Savy James for just as long. What was it about those James sisters that stole a Matthews boy's attention, and soon after, their hearts?

"Sav and Fox want a double wedding," Joe was saying. "We'll need you home."

"Yeah... yeah."

Will wasn't sure if his brother could hear the lack of enthusiasm in his voice. He'd made his visits back to the Flying Cross Ranch fewer and far between after he'd disappointed their father with his choices in life. The pang in his heart was still a real thing. Though when he saw the next act walk out onto the stage, his heart picked up a few beats.

"Will you be able to take time off from the airline?"

"Yeah… sure." Will was going to be able to take all the time he needed off from the airline, seeing as that was no longer his career path.

"There's so much to do, and we're going to need you," Joe was saying.

"Yeah… right."

The sultry songstress wrapped a slender hand around the microphone. Every man in the room leaned forward as her vibrant red lips came close to the mic. Will included. But he'd always leaned forward whenever she parted those lips in song, or just to say hello.

"You never know," said Joe, "by the time you get here, there might be three weddings. I wouldn't be surprised if Topher finds Tricksy and proposes."

That brought Will out of his stupor. He blinked once, twice. But his vision was still filled with the songbird on stage. She opened her mouth and the sweetest sounds began to fill the room.

"Hey, what's that playing in the background?"

"Oh, it's just the radio."

"It sounds like Tricksy singing. Where are you?"

"Joe, I gotta go. I'll talk to you soon."

Will hit disconnect before his brother could ask any more questions, or hear any more incriminating evidence. Namely, the fact that Will was seated at the back of a dive bar, in the shadows, listening to his brother's ex as she crooned a somebody-done-somebody-wrong love song.

Will knew the actors in this particular song. It was his brother Topher who had done Tricksy wrong. But the truth was, it wasn't Topher at all who had been the culprit. It had been Will. And Will could never let Tricksy find that out.

He could never seem to stay away from the woman for too long, either. And so he slunk down once more in the back and listened to the songbird that he would never catch because she was in love with his brother.

CHAPTER TWO

The butterflies had set up shop in her belly. They were old friends of Tricksy's. They came fluttering about every time she found herself at the back of a stage. She would've worried if they hadn't come with her.

They tickled her belly. They danced in her heart. They got choked up in her throat because they wanted to get out and get into the world. Much like the songs Tricksy wanted to sing. That's where the words to all her songs lived; in her belly, in her heart, all rising up to her chest wanting to burst out.

Tricksy took a deep breath, willing the winged creatures and her words to hold on just one more second. It was almost time for them to fly out of her and flit about the room, dazzling the audience with their color and beauty.

Tricksy shut her eyes and reached out her hands. Unfortunately, her palms came away empty. There was no Foxy at her right to grab hold of her hand. There was no Savy at her left to grab hold of the other.

She was alone. A solo act. Which was what she had thought she wanted.

Her older sister Savy had always been a spotlight hog with her alto voice. Savy often made it hard for Tricksy to harmonize her soprano voice with hers. After the last fight they had backstage, Savy had walked out the backstage door and never come back. Foxy had followed.

But that was fine. Tricksy was just fine. She had found harmony in her own voice. She didn't have to sing an octave lower. Now, on her own, she could hit those high notes.

Her cue came from the MC.

Tricksy took a deep breath, letting the butterflies and the words know they were about to take the spotlight. It was show time.

She stepped onto the stage. The first thing she noticed were the lights. It was hard not to. The stage lights were always blinding. It was hard for the performers to see the crowds. That's why once she stepped onto the stage, the butterflies fled. The insects were searching for flowers and nectar. Tricksy was a creature that sought the applause.

It greeted her the moment she stepped onto the stage. Not as loud as she would've liked. But this was a new crowd. She had to win them over if she wanted a more permanent spot here at Ronny's Dive.

Yes, Ronny had called his bar a dive. And it fit the definition. The food was fried to within an inch of its life so that customers couldn't tell that it was at the end of its shelf life. The bar top was sticky, and so were the floors. Likely because they were both cleaned with the exact same rag.

She'd sung in worse places when her mother was alive and shepherding her and her sisters' careers. Those dives had been in places where preteens should never have set foot in. Ronny's was a few steps up from that.

Tricksy navigated the sound cables in her heels and made her way to the microphone. Once there, she wrapped her fingers around the cold metal and came up close to the bulbous grid of the mic.

The music started. She opened her mouth, and the world fell away.

Tricksy found the note. She hopped on and rode the strings to the high pitch where she belonged.

It's you, my dear, whom I adore.

The song was a slow melody, perfect for her voice. She got in her trills and rolls -something she could never do when Savy's deep voice brought the performance down.

Divine worship for my devoted mon amore.

As she sang, Tricksy felt weightless. The higher her voice went as she sang a song about giving her heart away to her first and only love. It should break her heart to sing about Topher Matthews every time she got on stage. But her heart joyed in the song because it got to sing. Even if it was singing about the man who had spouted poetic words to her one day only to say the same thing to Judy Cartwright a few weeks later under the bleachers.

Tricksy poured all her angst and heartbreak into break up songs about Topher. If the songs ever made the radio, they would give Taylor Swift a run for her money.

Out in the audience, the women in the crowd appeared to feel the same way. They got up, throwing their hands in the air as Tricksy's voice rose higher. They swayed their bodies in time to the beat as she belted the notes out.

Clearly, these girls all had a Topher in their past. A gruff boy with a handsome smile. The kind she was sure just needed her tender loving care to pull him out of his bad boy ways.

Yeah, right. Last she'd heard of Topher, he was breaking hearts on other continents. His Instagram account showed that he'd left behind a trail in Afghanistan. There were tweets about his escapades in Germany. For a time, his name had been a trending hashtag on TikTok.

Not that she was stalking him or anything.

All girls reported the same lines he'd used on her. Telling them that she was a dear whom he adored. That his adoration was one of devotion for his life. But a few days later, he would inevitably show his true colors. Topher Matthews wasn't the passionate poet he pretended to be. He was a womanizing rake.

Tricksy hit the highest note of the song. She belted it out, using every last bit of the breath in her lungs. When she was through, she was met with raucous applause.

She took a bow. Not because of the gratitude for her audience. She bowed because she had nothing left in her. Her body simply collapsed in half.

A few deep breaths and she could stand again. She was herself again. The butterflies returned from their flight and settled back in her belly. Her words, now that they'd gotten out of her heart, out of her chest, went back inside her to relax until she called on them again.

That song always took it out of her. When she rose, the lights weren't so bright. She opened her eyes and saw a single face. The face of the owner. Ronny didn't look pleased.

His gaze narrowed at her. They'd talked about this. The customers weren't here for a sad, some-body done somebody wrong song. Most of the time, only the women would get up and dance.

A look out in the crowd told Tricksy that it was only women up on their feet. The men hung back, fidgeting and looking uncomfortable. Many looked at their watches, at their phones, and at the door.

Bars like this weren't about the art of the performers. The people came to shake off their blues, not be reminded of them. Customers came to dance. If they danced, they'd get thirsty. If they got thirsty, they'd get hungry. It was about the money, not the art Ronny had told her time and again. Which meant that Tricksy had to change her tune.

She raced to hop on the new beat the band played. The song was a Top Forties hit that could be heard all day on the radio. It was a song about shaking one's backside while wearing a trendy outfit. It was about finding company for just that night with no strings attached. They lyrics flew by fast, faster than the beat of butterfly wings. But Tricksy rode it out.

By the chorus, the men were out of their seats. People threw up their hands. They began to shimmy their bodies to the music. No one was listening to her voice anymore, just moving along to the beat. Which is why they were here.

It appeared everyone, men and women included, wanted what this song had to offer. Fashionably, free fun for just one night. This music had nothing to do with the vocalist. Anyone could sing the song. In fact, everyone was singing along. Her voice was drowned out as the crowd sang along.

Tricksy's high voice got lower and lower.

A man shimmied his large body up to the edge of the stage. He put his hand out as though asking her to dance. Tricksy demurred and moved to the other side of the stage. He followed, hand still out, insistent.

Tricksy backed up, but the man took a step onto the stage. His steps halted as he went tumbling back. There was another man behind the first, and Tricksy raised her fist again, ready to meet her next assailant.

Only to pause. She knew a Matthews when she saw him. Though this wasn't the Matthews she expected.

"Will?"

CHAPTER THREE

ill knew something was wrong when the music changed. He hadn't particularly enjoyed the lyrics to the song about his brother. Mainly because the words to the poem Topher had recited to win Tricksy over had been first butchered by Topher, then later butchered to unrecognizability in the song.

The dear that I adore

Devoted to mon amour.

Those were the original words. They'd been in church that morning all those years ago, which is the only reason Will could fathom Topher had tacked on the notion of worship and divinity. It had completely wrangled the rhyme of Will's verse. But as he hadn't been the one to deliver the words, he really couldn't be the one to complain.

Though Will did complain a week later when his brother further butchered his poem about Tricksy when Topher used it to steal a kiss from Judy Cartwright beneath the bleachers where everyone could see. Then everyone hastened to run and tell Tricksy, who had been inconsolable.

Will knew, because he'd been the shoulder she'd cried on. He'd wanted to tell her not to cry over his brother. He'd wanted to tell her that the words she'd thought belonged only to her, and not to Judy Cartwright, and later Bess Goodman, and then a little later beyond that Delia Thomas, had been written expressly for her. By him.

But Will knew telling Tricksy the whole truth would bring her nothing but even more pain. As a conflict avoider, Will wasn't willing to take that step. But also as the man in love with Tricksy, he couldn't bear the thought of causing her a single second of upset.

For the past few years, Will had found Tricksy in the dive bars she'd performed in and sat in the back and listened to her voice. The places had gotten seedier and seedier as the years had gone by. But her voice always rang true. Except for right now.

This song wasn't her. She wasn't a pop singer. Nothing Tricksy James did was in line with the synthesizing and syncopated beats of a Top Forties song because she was far too unique to even be considered on that list.

He'd watched her face as she sang. All of the joy had seeped out of Tricksy's eyes as she'd bopped to the beat. The notes fell flat to his ears. But the people around him continued to dance and sing along, further muting her voice.

Will stood to leave. In all his years of checking in on Tricksy, she had never once caught him lurking in the background. Now, with this upbeat tune that belied her voice, he didn't want her to catch him baring witness to the scene.

This wasn't the life she'd told him she wanted all those years ago. She was settling, something she told him she'd never do. Something he himself had never done.

Except when it came to her.

Will had settled for her friendship when he'd wanted her soul. He'd settled for her kindness when he'd wanted her passion. And now he was turning his back on her when she was clearly in distress.

He turned back and was instantly enthralled by her face as she sang. She might not enjoy the words she was singing, but she loved singing. The sight made Will eager to do something he said he'd never do again. He wanted to give Tricksy his words to sing.

Tricksy's gumption had inspired Will to stick to his own guns. He was the only Matthews boy who hadn't gone into the service. But he still had his wings.

Flying commercial airplanes had given him a sense of belonging in his family of Air Force pilots. Like all his brothers, Will loved soaring high. The possibility of shooting an enemy down had never sat well with him. Instead, he spent his time getting people safely where they needed to go for work, for pleasure, for family.

His downtime between flights allowed him to pursue his hobby of poetry. The poems had piled up over the years. Until he'd had enough to publish in a book. His debut would be releasing soon and Will would be hanging up his wings for a new career.

The weight of his decision forced him back down in his chair. If he'd had the courage to reach for a dream he never considered making come true, perhaps now was the time to reach for the woman that had always been there when he'd closed his eyes.

Will sat in the darkness of the club and listened to the only woman he'd ever loved sing a song about having a one-night stand. He had just about had enough when a guy approached the stage and began to get handsy.

Will looked over to the security. The buff guy who had manned the door was now eying a girl in a miniskirt who looked far too young to be in here. He was not paying the artist on stage any mind. Nor the fan that was too attentive.

The bartender was filling drinks. A man off to the side in a suit, who looked like he might own the dismal dive, was all smiles at the performance on and off the stage. He looked like he was in no hurry to come to the songstress's aid. In fact, he looked like he approved of the show.

That was enough for Will. He couldn't leave Tricksy in distress. Will rose from his table.

He made his way through the writhing bodies on the dance floor. More than one woman tried to sway him into a dance. Will sidestepped them all until he reached his target.

He tapped the guy on his shoulder. The man didn't even turn to glance at Will. His hands were still trying to grab at Tricksy who fought him off while still maintaining her pitch.

Will felt anger boil up in him. It was short lived as all anger was with him. In the foster care system, he'd always managed to stay invisible. In a house full of alpha males, he was never bothered to take a back seat. He knew from the short time he spent with his parents in North Korea that if one person fought, the entire family would be hurt. His father had fought back and his mother had been killed for his efforts.

Words were the best weapons in situations like these. Will's fist unfurled and came to hang loosely by his side. Yet somehow, the burly man went tumbling back.

Will stepped aside to let the man fall to the ground. He looked up to find Tricksy's fist extended. Just as everyone knew not to cross a Matthews boy, or a Silver sister, high up there was the warning to never, ever, cross a James girl.

The bar descended into chaos as the music stopped and the man flailed on the filthy floor. Tricksy's eyes landed on him.

"Will?"

She reached for him. Will caught her up, lifting her down off the stage and into his arms. She stared up at him in wonder. For a brief moment, Will experienced a moment of nirvana. He had everything in his life that he'd ever coveted right here in his arms.

"Is Topher here?" she asked.

And then it all came crashing down at the mention of his brother's name.

CHAPTER FOUR

Tricksy's voice felt hollow. Her chest felt empty and her soul weary. It was mostly from the song that had been shoved down her throat. But that didn't account for her sore hand. The skin at her knuckles smarted where she'd connected with the handsy man wanting a private dance.

It should've been evident to him that she wasn't *that* kind of performer. For one, she had on all her clothes. For two, she could hit the high notes without a synthesizer. But all Mr. Handsy heard was another person's lyrics which, to his brain, suggested that he could shoot his shot.

Well, if you shoot your shot at a country girl, raised by a drug addicted mother, who'd grown up in foster care, you would get exactly what you deserved. And that was lying flat on your backside with your meaty hand clutching at your bloody nose.

Somewhere in the midst of the indignation and the ache in her hand, Tricksy felt like she was floating. She felt secure. Safe. Protected. Cared for.

There was a delightful smell of spice that made her feel rejuvenated. Spice and something musty, like old books. Its mix of scents reminded her of home. The only home that had been a constant in her life. The Bright Horizons Foster Care.

But that couldn't be right. Bright Horizons smelled of harsh chemicals that didn't quite mask the unclean smell of bedwetters and unwashed bodies. Though there had been a few books on a shelf in the common room. One person had always been sitting on the floor beneath those shelves with his nose in a book.

That's what she was smelling. That corner and the boy at the bookshelf. She'd had a few hugs from that boy when she was feeling down. He always seemed to be there when she was sad and needed a shoulder.

Tricksy was wrapped up in someone's arms now. But this was a man's arms. Not a boy's. Still, there was no mistaking the scent of him. No mistaking the feel of Will Matthews.

A memory of leaning into Will hit her mind. Topher had forgotten about a date they'd planned. He'd kept her waiting for a half hour, but Will had been there. He'd sat next to her and allowed her to lean on him. At some point, he'd wrapped an arm around her and they sat just like that.

Will had always given the best hugs. He was gentle, but strong. The kind of man a girl could trust.

In reality, Will Matthews was a unicorn. He wasn't the kind of man that songs were written about. Because no one would ever believe he was real.

But he was. And he was holding onto Tricksy, giving her his magical strength and quiet comfort.

In that comfort, there was one thing Tricksy knew. Wherever Will was, Topher was not far behind. The two of them had been inseparable in their youth. Though Tricksy had always suspected that it was Will who attached himself to Topher's hip. Because where Topher always managed to find trouble that he would solve with his fists, Will's calm head would always prevail by talking the offended party down until a peace treaty was reached… or long enough for his other brothers to join the fray.

"Is Topher here?"

Will's hold loosened on her. But not before it tightened for a brief second. Or maybe that was Tricksy's imagination?

"No," Will said, releasing his hold on her. "It's just me."

There was a hint of resignation in his voice. But that had always been there. Will was the quietest of the Matthews boys. Always keeping to the shadows. It was no wonder he'd latched onto Topher, who was loud and talkative.

Tricksy had always liked sitting next to Will at the foster care dinner table. She never had to say anything to him. She never had to make her voice louder than his, like she had to do with her sisters. It had been so long since she'd had a moment of quiet.

"You broke my nose!"

The shout didn't come from the floor because the handsy private dancer was stumbling to his feet. He reached for Tricksy. Before she could put up her dukes to deliver another deserving blow, she was tucked out of the way and behind Will's back.

Mr. Handsy threw a punch. That punch would've

landed right at Will's right eye. But in his quiet and careful way, Will simply stepped aside. The punch flew through air and the momentum sent Mr. Handsy crashing down into a table full of guests and drinks.

Glass splattered to the floor. The table gave out under his weight and split in two. Girls screamed as their dresses were doused with cheap alcohol. Guys leaped out of the way as their pristine, expensive sneakers were threatened by the brown liquid and fruity concoctions.

"That's it, James. You're outta here!"

Tricksy whirled around to face Ronny. She opened her mouth to protest, to fight. But all the fight had gone out of her. Mainly because her throat was still sore from belting out the hit song. The truth was, Tricksy wanted to get out of there.

She reached out to the left, but Foxy wasn't there to take her hand. She reached out to the right, but Savy was nowhere to be found. She took a step back and a strong arm came around her.

Will's forearm pulled her into his strong chest. He shifted his weight and pulled her into his side. Tricksy's body sagged into his, letting him take all her weight as he gave her his strength.

She was done being strong. She was done lifting

her chin up and pretending everything was okay. She was done doing it on her own.

This had been her last shot at a break. She was low on funds. She wasn't going to get paid for tonight. Ronny would surely deduct this destruction of his property from her cut, and she was likely to owe more since she was being paid so low.

She had no idea what to do. But right now it didn't matter, because she wasn't the one holding herself up. It was Will. And once again, like when she had had her spirit broken, he let her lean on him.

CHAPTER FIVE

*W*ill kept a hand around Tricksy's waist as they made their way to the back of the club to get her things. He slung her travel bag over his shoulder, noticing how light the bag was. He said nothing to her about it. As a frequent flyer himself, he'd learned the art of packing only the essentials. But he would admit, his carryon was twice as heavy as Tricksy's pink rolling duffle bag.

Instead of commenting on it, he carried the excess baggage on his back, and he reached for her with his free hand. Tricksy came willingly. She seemed too dazed and exhausted to protest. She hadn't said another word after being fired from the dive bar. Will hadn't seen her this silent since the day Topher broke up with her.

Just as she had that fateful day, Tricksy rested her head against Will's chest. Her steps matched his as they crossed the threshold out the back door. The moon was high in the sky. The night filled with the sound of revelry that came from Friday night fun seekers. When they came to a stop at a streetlight in the parking lot, Tricksy shut her eyes to the yellow spotlight.

That's when he knew all wasn't well. For any James sister to turn away from a spotlight meant that something was wrong. "Tricks?"

Tricksy let out a long, low sigh. The sound was weary and off key. It came from somewhere deep in her belly. When she was done, her shoulders slumped as though she'd emptied her body of every last bit of breath she'd carried for a while.

"Tricks, you okay?"

She didn't lift her head. She didn't open her eyes. She took in another deep breath, and let it out long and low like the first one. She looked defeated.

"Hey, don't let that jerk get you down. You're too good for this place. I'm sure you have other gigs lined up."

She snorted at that. "No one else wants me."

The reply was on the tip of his tongue."

"All the clubs want a pop singer in a mini-skirt. That's not me."

No, it wasn't her. Tricksy was a fan of the 1940s era pin-up girl. Many of her dresses now and when she was younger had a cinched waist with a flaring skirt. The striped dress she wore tonight brought the eye down to her long legs. Even though they were covered from her waist down to her calves, it still let the mind wonder.

Her hair was always in curls pinned atop her head. The swoops and lulls of her lustrous hair would make a man dizzy if he followed the curves around her head. Her lipstick was always a vibrant red that gave a man ideas that weren't always gentlemanly.

Not Will. He had been raised a gentleman. He averted his gaze from Tricksy's mouth and looked her in the eye. Her gaze was watery, but not a single tear had spilled. That left her dark eye liner giving her catlike eyes an even more exaggerated flare. It was her lips that still slanted downward into a frown.

The sight only served to make his heart squeeze.

He could never stand to see this woman sad. Which is why he fed his brother the lines that he knew would make Tricksy's romantic heart smile.

Will had often come to her rescue when they were younger. Oftentimes when his brother forgot about a date he'd made with her. Having a girlfriend hadn't ranked high on Topher's everyday to do list.

Tricksy was the first thing Will thought of each morning that he woke up. She was his last thought every night. Even now, he thought about her at least every ten minutes throughout the day. Her happiness and contentment meant more to Will than his own. So, when he realized that Tricksy only had eyes for his brother, Will decided that she would have him.

"Let me take you home," he said to her now. "Where do you live?"

That rattled her. She stepped away from him. She looked up at him, but not directly into his eyes. She looked at his ears.

Will had quietly studied Tricksy all of his younger years. He knew that that look, that slight avoidance of meeting his eyes, meant she was about to skirt the truth.

"I'm between places right now," she said.

"Where are you headed next?"

"I don't have a gig lined up. But I should be getting a call soon." She focused on his other ear.

From that, Will knew she was both homeless and without any prospects. He racked his brain trying to figure out away to give her money without it seeming like charity. With them both being foster kids, he knew how much she loathed the idea of a hand out.

"Wait, Will?" She met his eyes then. One of her catlike eyes lifted, as though she was taking him in for the first time tonight. "What are you doing here?"

Will's gaze slipped to Tricksy's right ear. "I was on a layover. I was looking through the local paper's entertainment section for something to do, and saw your name on a billboard and decided to come see an old friend."

That was mostly true. He was on a layover, but only because he specifically looked up where she was performing and got on that particular flight rotation.

"Where are you flying off to next?"

Will glanced at her other ear. "Home."

"You're headed back to Flying Cross?"

"My presence has been requested. I'm sure yours has been, too."

"Why?" Tricksy's hand landed on his chest in a

jerky motion. "What's happened? I thought your dad was okay."

Haran Matthews had suffered a heart attack a couple months ago. The old man had overworked himself out on the ranch by himself. But now he had a full house of orphans and foster kids to help shoulder the work, thanks to Joe and Savy moving the Bright Horizons Foster Care Home into the Matthews' old bunkhouse.

"Dad's okay."

The relief on her face was instant. Tricksy's hand fell away from his chest. Will had to stop himself from catching her wrist and holding her hand there.

"I'm headed back for the wedding," Will continued.

"Which of the Silver sisters is getting married this time?"

"They're all married."

"No kidding?"

"It's your sisters' wedding."

Tricksy blinked. "Charlie and Savy are finally gonna do it, huh?"

"I said sisters, plural. Charlie and Savy and Joe and Foxy."

Again, Tricksy blinked.

"They didn't tell you?"

Tricksy looked down. With that look, it appeared that no one had. The next words out of Will's mouth shocked them both.

"Come home with me."

Tricksy watched Will's lips move as he formed the words. There were tons of words coming from his lips. Words like *married, sisters, home.*

Instead of focusing on the words he was saying, she chose to focus on Will's mouth. Will had nice lips. Not the thin lips he'd had as a child. Or at least she thought they were thin? Had she noticed?

No, she definitely hadn't. Because if she had, she would've seen how plump Will's lips were. The top one was perfectly symmetrical on both sides as it formed the top part of a heart.

No, not a heart. A bow string. Because Will was a Matthews. Those boys were all warriors to their core. Fighters ready to step into battle.

Except Will. Will had never been the first to run into a fight. But he had done a lot of talking. Talking with that mouth. And those lips.

She would've noticed that bottom lip. It was as plush as a pillow. Not a motel room pillow that she was used to sleeping in for these past few years. No, it would've been a five-star hotel pillow that stayed plump and firm even after someone flounced back onto it.

Will's bottom lip looked sturdy enough for a woman to fling herself at him. He'd catch her with that bottom lip. Trap her in the bow of his top lip. And hold her securely.

Tricksy shook her head. Firstly, because what the heck was she doing waxing poetic about Will Matthews's lips? But secondly, and most importantly, she did not wax poetic. She wrote angsty songs of heartbreak and loss at the hands of Mr. Wrong. Not flowery ballads of kissing Mr. Good Guy.

And Will Matthews was definitely Mr. Good Guy. He was *the* good guy. Mr. Good Guy with some seriously kissable lips. She would be willing to bet a lot of women appreciated the way those lips would move across theirs.

But no. Will wasn't a player. He likely had a

steady girlfriend even now. One he would never consider cheating on. One who was likely missing having his kissable lips pressed against hers.

Topher was an excellent kisser. Tricksy had thoroughly enjoyed the way his lips had moved across hers. But she couldn't remember what his lips looked like. She was having trouble even grasping exactly what they felt like. Even though she sang about how his lips had done her wrong in her songs.

Had Topher's lips been thin or heart-shaped like Will's? Had they been wide like Will's or just a small slash in his face? Tricksy couldn't remember. How could she not remember her one true love's lips?

"Tricks? Do you want to come home with me?"

There were so many emotions roiling around in Tricksy's head and in her heart. Home? Did she want to go home? She hadn't been home in over a year. And the last time she was there, she'd fought with her sister Savy.

And now Savy was getting married. That wasn't a surprise. Savy and Charlie Matthews had been engaged since they were twelve. What was a surprise was Foxy's engagement. And to Joe Matthews, of all people?

Whereas Savy and Tricksy had been engaged in a silent war, Foxy had been in contact with Tricksy.

Foxy had failed to mention she was even dating Joe, much less marrying the guy.

Foxy had declared herself Switzerland in the cold war between her two older sisters. But Tricksy supposed now her younger sister had chosen sides, and once again Tricksy been left to go it alone.

Will reached a hand to her forearm. His strong fingers wrapped around her flesh and squeezed. With just that singular touch, Tricksy felt instant relief.

It had always been like this with Will. He'd always brought her comfort. Topher didn't like dealing with her emotions, and Tricksy James was an emotional woman.

Her ex always tapped his foot when she tried to have a heart to heart with him. He'd constantly tried to change the subject when she wanted to discuss her feelings.

But Will? Will would always listen intently to her every emotion, be it happiness or sorrow.

"You don't have to go," Will was saying.

He pulled her in for another hug. Tricksy didn't protest the affection. She felt like a well that had been empty for years. Will was filling her to the brim with just his presence.

"I'll fly you wherever you want to go," he said.

Tricksy didn't want to go anywhere. She wanted to stay wrapped up in Will's embrace. A funny thought settled in her scrambled brain. That thought was that Will Matthews, with his spicy-musty-book scent and his huggalicious arms, was as good as being at home.

"I want to go home," she said.

Will squeezed tighter. Tricksy did the same. They stood like that for long moments.

Tricksy pulled back to look at him. She had to blink a couple of times. In her memories, Will still had baby fat around his cheeks. That was gone and what was left was chiseled features. A strong jaw. Two compassionate eyes. And those kissable lips.

She gave herself another shake. At this rate, she should worry about getting brain damage with all the shaking going on. In her mind, the image of Will blipped between him as a kid and him as a man. When she looked back up at him, only the man remained.

Tricksy stepped out of his embrace.

Will shoved his hands into his pockets. The movement brought attention to his chest. There had been no definition there when he was a kid or a teen. He'd been scrawny and malnourished. She remembered the day he'd arrived at the foster home.

Soon after, he and his grandfather had escaped with their lives from North Korea. Will had lost his parents to the regime. A few weeks in America, and he'd lost his grandfather, too.

He'd been nothing but skin and bones back then. He hadn't known much English. But when a book had been placed in his hands, he'd gobbled up the language and soon spoke it better than all the other kids who'd been born in the country.

That skinny kid with little to say was a thing of the past. Will Matthews was all defined muscles and sure words now. A solid chest poked against the front of his shirt, stringing the buttons. A six pack poked at the bottom of his shirt just above his buckle. And those lips kept saying the most comforting things to her.

"Topher will probably be coming home soon for the weddings."

And now her ex was added into the mix. Well, at the worst-case scenario, she needed to write some new songs. And the artist who suffered was the one who made the most beautiful art.

CHAPTER SEVEN

Their suitcases lay side by side. Neither were large. Both would easily pass the new carryon regulations airplanes gave for luggage stored in the overhead compartments.

Most of Tricksy's life had been as a performer on the road. Will knew she was fond of both clothes and shoes. It awed him, at the same time as it worried him, that her life had been reduced down to the size of a carryon.

For Will, this was a necessity of his job as a commercial airline pilot. His former job as a commercial airline pilot. He'd have to get used to saying that.

He waited for the twinge of loss to come at having to hang up his wings. His pulse was steady at the thought. His heart jumped at the sharp, unexpected turn his life was now taking. Especially in light of the passenger he handed into the seat beside him.

Will slid his suitcase over a nudge, giving Tricksy's prime real estate in the trunk of his car. He took a moment to stare down at the two vessels laying side by side. Her pink case and his utilitarian black case. They did not look like they belonged together, but they fit snuggly one beside the other.

Before he'd pulled onto the main road, Tricksy's eyes had closed. She'd been out like a light before they'd turned onto the highway. Will had been hoping to talk to her, to catch up, to simply listen to the sound of her voice.

He made sure to hide the CD recording she'd made of her demo years ago. Even though the disc was years old and well traveled, it had not a single scratch on the surface. Despite being played on a daily basis.

As Will drove into the darkness of night, he couldn't help but notice the bags under Tricksy's eyes. She hadn't been sleeping well. The only time he'd seen any life in her eyes had been when she was up on the stage singing about her heartbreak over his brother.

It troubled him that she still carried the burden of that pain all these years later. He'd once read in a *Cosmo* article that the time it took to get over a breakup was the duration of the relationship plus half. By that calculation, Tricksy should've been over Topher years ago. The entirety of the affair had barely lasted a couple of months.

Despite all of her assurances that she was fine, Will knew that she still suffered. The joy and satisfaction at seeing her last night and hearing her sing dissipated under the burden of her sadness. It was a weight he could not bear. He knew what he had to do.

At the next exit, Will pulled over at a rest stop. The gravel under the wheels was loud to his ears as the car came to a slow stop. The gentle hum of tractor trailer engines made his ear drums ache when he pulled the keys from the ignition.

A glance at Tricksy showed she still slept fitfully. That was a good thing. He didn't want her to witness what he was about to do.

Stepping out of the car, Will put a good bit of distance between himself and his car. Though he didn't go so far that Tricksy was out of his line of sight. He pulled out his cellphone and tapped his favorites contacts. His father held spot number one. Will tapped on number two.

He had to hit redial a couple of times to escape the voice message. Finally, on the third try, Topher picked up.

"Do you have any idea what time it is over here?" came his brother's gruff reply.

Topher Matthews was not a morning person. He wasn't a night person either. The man could catnap all day if left to his own devices. Which served him as a soldier; the ability to grab rest whenever there was downtime, and be wide awake during every other hour of the day.

"I need you to come home," said Will.

"I already told Charlie that I'll try and get time off for the wedding. But I can't guarantee it."

Topher's voice was gruff with sleep. But it sounded like he was pulling the phone away from his face with those last words. Which could mean that he thought the conversation was over and he was about to hang up.

"Toph," Will called into the line. When he realized he'd raised his voice, he raised his head. But Tricksy hadn't stirred in the passenger seat. "It's not for Charlie and Sav."

"Yeah, I know. Joe and Foxy are getting married,

too." Topher's voice was louder, letting Will know that he hadn't put the phone down. Unfortunately, it was now even more disgruntled.

"Not for them either. For Tricksy."

There was a pause. Followed by a grumble in the shape of a sigh. "Tricksy's getting married?"

There was a pang in Will's heart at that notion of Tricksy getting married. Will knew Tricksy could never be his, not when her heart belonged to his brother. But he had never thought through the idea of her being completely off limits once some other man put a ring on her finger.

"No," said Will. "She's not getting married. She's coming home."

Another unintelligible grumble sounded from the receiver. There was a ruffle of sheets. At least Will now had his brother's full attention.

"I think it would do her good to see you," said Will.

"Why? She hates my guts."

"She doesn't hate you." Will pressed his lips together before uttering his next words. "I think she's still in love with you."

There was silence on the other end of the line. Will thought Topher might've hung up. Or fallen back asleep.

"We both know that's not possible," came Topher's reply. "I'm not the man she thinks I am."

"But you could be."

"No, I couldn't be. Because it's you."

Now it was Will's turn to let out a low sigh. Though his sigh sounded less like a bear prematurely woken from hibernation, and more like a bear trying to catch a salmon swimming upstream.

"Why don't you just tell her the truth, bro. Tell her that it was you that wrote those poems. It was you who told me what to say. It's you that she fell in love with. I was just your stand in."

"Toph-"

"I'm not gonna be your Serious de Burke anymore."

"Cyrano de Bergerac. And you would've been Christian, the man Roxanne was in love with."

"Whatever. I'm not doing it. I don't want to be in a relationship. I'm not cut out for them."

"That's not true."

The silence on the other end of the line was pointed. Will could swear he saw Topher's brow raise on the cellphone's face.

"You're a great guy," Will said.

"Yeah, I know. And so do a lot of women. I'd like

to keep it that way. Go put your big nose in somebody else's love life. Preferably your own."

"Did you just call me big nose?"

"Are you gonna keep pretending to be a man unworthy of love?"

"Wow, Toph, that was kind of poetic."

"It's what you get when you pull me out of a good dream. I'm hanging up on you and going back to sleep. Go tell Roxanne how you feel, Big Nose."

And with that, Topher hung up the phone.

For long moments, all Will could do was stare down at the device. His sole obstacle for telling Tricksy his true feelings had been removed. He could march up to the car, wake her from her dreams, and tell her that his heart was hers.

CHAPTER EIGHT

Tricksy had slept in many a car over the course of her career. She'd fought her sisters over seats in their mom's beat up Chevy when they were kids traveling on the road. The fight was always over the right back passenger seat because the left back passenger seat had a spring loose in the side of the seat.

She'd rock, paper, scissored who would get night driving duty when she and her sisters were a singing trio. She'd hurried onto discount buses, aiming for a seat just a few rows behind the middle where she wouldn't hear the door opening and closing of the main door with each stop, and she would be far enough away from the bathroom and wouldn't get a whiff of something unpleasant as she tried to slumber.

Car sleeping had always been a chore. But this ride was the smoothest she'd ever been on. When the sun tickled her cheek from the passenger side window, she came to wakefulness slowly, eagerly, without a crick in her neck or a protest in her spine. She felt absolutely rejuvenated, like she'd slept on a thousand count sheets in a five-star hotel.

Even better, this hotel had room service. The smell of eggs and bacon greeted her nose, along with the aroma of a strong brewed cup of coffee. Tricksy wondered if she'd died and gone to heaven at some point on the highway.

"Good morning."

A comfortable cushion, a delectable breakfast, and the gentlest wake up call any girl could ask for? Yes, this was heaven. Will Matthews smiled at her from the driver's seat. His gaze on her was observant and kind. Never leering or calculating. The woman who caught Will's heart would never have hers broken. No, she'd always have a strong and comfortable set of arms to hold her, kind words whispered in her ear, and an attentive man to see to her every need.

Lucky girl.

"We're home."

Tricksy looked out the car window as Will set the food on her lap. Sure enough, she saw the small town of Honor Valley. The town's main street was bustling with a crowd of at least ten people walking on either side of the road. The tallest building was only three stories high, nothing like the skyscrapers of the major cities she'd toured in. Pedestrians waited at the crosswalk while trucks came to a full stop to let them cross without need of a flashing sign.

There was the pizza parlor where she and her sisters would sing for change on the street.

There was the ice cream shop their mom had taken them to and left them one time when she went to score and forgot her maternal duties.

There was the one-screen movie theater where she and Topher had their first date.

"You okay, Tricks?"

"Yeah." Before Will could ask her anymore questions, Tricksy took a sip of coffee and then gave the most pleasurable sigh in her life. "It's perfect."

It was an honest answer. The coffee was perfect. A strong, light brown roast with one cream and four sugars.

"A little bit of coffee with your sugar," said Will. "I remember."

He did indeed. And since he'd put at least half a cup of sugar in the beverage, Tricksy wouldn't have to be embarrassed about how much she put in.

"We got in a little late and I figured they'd be finished with breakfast at the ranch and out doing chores. I didn't want you to starve while you waited for lunch."

"Thanks, Will. That was thoughtful."

But that was Will. Always thoughtful. Always attentive.

Whereas she'd been a bad friend. Every time Topher had disappointed her, Will had been there. Yet she hadn't once thought to reach out to him after their breakup all those years ago.

Well, that was ending now. She needed a friend like Will in her life. She needed to be a friend.

She just wasn't sure how to go about it? Every man who'd come into her life always wanted something from her. Usually something she wasn't willing to give. Will had never asked her for anything. What could she possibly give him?

"Tricks... there's something I've been meaning to tell you."

"Yeah?" she asked when the silence stretched. But her attention was diverted to a billboard across the street on the door of the local bar. There was an announcement for the bar's regular talent night. "I can't believe they still have that."

On those nights, the twenty-one and over bar allowed families and young children onto the stools to sample the town's talents. Fond memories hit Tricksy of her and her sisters singing in the show. She and her sisters always got the most applause when they sang together. Tricksy had even done a few solo acts on that stage. It was where she'd debuted the breakup ballad about Topher.

At first she'd been met with stunned silence. Likely because everyone in the audience knew who the song was about. But on the last note, the crowd - of mostly women- were on their feet.

Tricksy had insisted on including the song in their act. Savy had scoffed. They sang upbeat, happy songs. Lots of show tunes that catered to her alto voice. But Tricksy had gotten a taste of what it felt like to have applause for her own creation, and she wanted more of the accolades.

It was around that time that she and her sisters had performed together less and less. It had also been the time when she'd been going through her breakup with Topher and she didn't want to sing any happy songs.

"You're thinking about him, aren't you?"

Tricksy turned back to Will. She knew she didn't have to clarify who. Not with Will. He'd been there through all of it.

But the truth was, Tricksy hadn't been thinking about Topher. Not really. That breakup was always somewhere near the front of her mind. Today that particular dissolution wasn't what caused the pang in her heart.

"I think I've been on my own too long," she said.

"You do?"

"I think it's time I do something about that."

"Really?"

"Yeah." Tricksy turned from the bar and the old memories. She faced Will. There was a light in his eyes and a smile full of expectation on his face. Seemed he was happy with her decision as well. "I'm gonna work on my relationship with my sisters."

"Oh?" Will blinked and his smile wobbled.

Tricksy cringed. She'd done it again. She'd leaned in on Will's shoulder and went on and on about her problems, when he'd wanted to talk to her about something.

"I'm sorry, Will. What was it you wanted to tell me?"

"That we should get a move on if we want to make it to the ranch before sundown."

CHAPTER NINE

He hadn't blown it. Will had to stop thinking that. He just had to find the perfect way to tell her his feelings. Along with the fact that he'd coached Topher all those years ago.

The moment sitting parked on Main Street had not been that moment. Not with all the memories of her past and his coming out of the shadows and into the sunlight at every street corner.

His words could wait. They could wait because right now, Tricksy was singing. She'd finished her breakfast and coffee and was now singing along to the radio.

She'd turned on an old, jazzy station on the car's radio. Tricksy's voice drowned out the accomplished singer who had sold out stadium seating.

They were now her background singer as she took center stage in the passenger seat of his car. He only wished he could record this impromptu performance right now and play it back for the rest of his days.

Tricksy bopped in her seat, shimmying her shoulders. Her voice was light and airy as though she had no care in the world. Like the past that had weighed on her shoulders only moments ago had flitted away like a kaleidoscope of butterflies.

He drove in the slow lane and took the long route home. Tricksy didn't seem to mind. He doubted she even noticed. All too soon, the sight of the Flying Cross Ranch came into view.

The place looked the same, but different in the noonday sun. The porch needed a fresh coat of paint. There were a few pieces of wood missing from the fence in the north pasture. Though the bunkhouse looked as though it had gotten some care since his time there.

Will knew that that's where the new batch of foster kids was staying. The five kids living there were a mixed bunch. In race and ethnicity like he and his brothers, but also in gender. That had been a sore spot when Charlie and Joe had tried to get their adoptive parents to also adopt the James girls.

Will never knew why his parents wouldn't budge on the matter. But they never turned the girls away when they came by.

Now, two James girls would live on the ranch, becoming Matthews themselves. And the third was coming to stay for a time. If Will had his way, Tricksy would have a permanent place on the ranch -a place at his side.

Looking up at the big house, Will expected to see his father and brothers out in the pastures, but there was no one in sight. He knew they had to be here because he saw his father's old truck in the drive. Perhaps they were all in the house for a late lunch?

Rounding the car, Will handed Tricksy out. She wrapped her fingers around his, pressing their palms together. The jolt went all the way through his body on down to his toes. He kept hold of her fingers as she stepped into the rich soil in her heels. As they climbed the porch steps, he didn't neglect the fact that their fingers were still entwined.

Tricksy squeezed his hand as though he were a lifeline. She was likely nervous to see her sisters again. Will would take that. He would be her strength now. He would lend it to her indefinitely.

He opened the door and was met with even more silence. It was odd. The house had always been filled with noise. And now that there were new foster kids here, it should be even louder than when he and his brothers were boys.

No sooner had Will had the thought, then a chorus of shouts rang out from every corner of the house.

"Surprise!"

Will clutched Tricksy to his chest. They both looked around wildly at the people who materialized from the stairs, the hall, and the kitchen. There were only a few faces that Will recognized; namely his father's old wizened face and his brother, Joe.

There were a handful of kids that eyed them skeptically. The kids were indeed made up of all shapes, sizes, and colors. There was a brown-skinned girl with long braids hanging over her shoulders. Her gaze was the most skeptical as she eyed Will and Tricksy. The other three kids were boys. The tallest fairly glared at the two of them. While the dark-haired one and the blond haired one looked on in awe. Not at Will, at Tricksy, who he still held firmly and securely in his arms.

"OMG, I knew it!"

That came from Foxy.

"I saw this," she said as she materialized from

behind a closet door. She pointed a finger at Will and Tricksy. "Didn't I tell you I saw this, Joe?"

"Will, what are you two doing here?" asked Joe. "We weren't expecting you for days. We weren't expecting you at all, Tricks."

In his arms, Tricksy bristled. If they weren't expecting them, then who had they shouted surprise for?

"I was expecting you," said Foxy, grabbing her sister's hands. But Tricksy didn't let go of Will. "I saw you two together in one of my visions a few days ago. Actually, it was years ago, but you -in real life- were so convinced that you were in love with Topher. But, you know what, to tell you the truth, I was convinced my true love was someone else when it was Joe all along. So, this makes total sense, doesn't it?"

Tricksy looked at Will. Will looked at Joe. They all looked at Foxy.

Will had forgotten how trying it could be to follow Foxy when she spoke. Especially when she spoke about her psychic abilities. Even more especially when Foxy only got her predictions right about half the time. Will that hoped this was one of those times she was half right.

"Now we all three can get married," Foxy was

saying. "Can you picture it? All three Jameses on a stage again. Well, an altar. It'll be epic."

Tricksy let go of Will's hand then. She clasped onto her sister's hands at those words. Will wanted to clasp onto Foxy's hands at that sentiment. Because he could picture it; he could picture himself at the altar with Tricksy.

Will looked at his father. The old man watched the scene play out with his trademark look of quiet contemplation. Will ached to know his father's true thoughts about this matter.

"Wait?" said Foxy. "Am I getting ahead of myself? Has Will even popped the question yet?"

Tricksy opened her mouth, but no words came out. Will wanted to fill the silence.

"You do know he's always been in love with you, right?" Foxy continued.

Tricksy turned to Will with wide eyes. Will's first instinct was to deny it. But it was the truth.

"Oh, no. It looks like he hasn't. So you won't be getting married with us. Such a shame," Foxy sighed. "I was all ready for the James sisters to be a trio again."

Behind them, the door opened again. Savy and Charlie entered with a little girl between them. Everyone scrambled to shout surprise again, but the effect was disjointed. The little girl didn't seem to care. She bolted into the house and jumped into Father Matthews' arms.

"Tricksy?" said Savy. "What are you doing here? And Will, is that you?"

"Yes," said Tricksy, coming to stand by Will's side and taking his hand. "We're here together. We're… together."

CHAPTER TEN

he show must go on. That was the saying in show business. It was a saying Fanny James often slurred after she'd fallen off the stage, or was bowing down to the porcelain gods when the drugs were running rampant in her system.

Though none of her daughters had much respect for their mother, they did have respect for that rule. And so, despite the unexpected guests showing up, despite the botched surprise, as well as the surprising new relationship that was unveiled, the show had to go on.

But this wasn't Tricksy and Will's show. It was the little girl, Daria's, show.

Tricksy hadn't met Daria the last time she'd come home, when Savy and Foxy were still living in the

Bright Horizons Foster Home. She hadn't met any of this new batch of kids who all must have arrived sometime within the last year.

Daria, who was the youngest of the new foster kids, had been taken away from Savy some time ago. After a legal battle with the state home, and the finalization of adoption paperwork of Daria's older brother, the kid was finally able to return to her forever home.

A twinge knotted in Tricksy's belly. Someplace deeper than where the butterflies lay in rest. She'd never had a home to call her own. Her early life had been far too unstable for that.

Like her sisters, Tricksy had dreamed of coming to live at the Flying Cross Ranch, marrying one of the Matthews, and never leaving. That dream was coming true for Savy and Foxy. It was even coming true for all these new foster kids.

Once again, Tricksy would be the odd one out. Left to fly solo after her brief gig here. And because this wasn't the Tricksy show, she had to step aside and let the light shine on the little girl.

As everyone showered love and praise on Daria, Savy kept sneaking furtive glances at Tricksy and Will. Tricksy did not let go of Will's hand. Not for a single second. She was sure if she did that, Savy would see through the whole thing.

Tricksy didn't understand her need to impress her sister. To show Savy that she was her equal. And, in a lot of instances, to one up her.

No, wait. Tricksy did know why. It was because of that brow of Savy's. She raised it like it was the kind of armor that could pierce into the person it was aimed at. And it was always aimed at Tricksy.

Tricksy felt her knees knocking under her sister's stare. Her upper lip quivered under the weight of the lie she'd told. Her bottom lip was about to spill all. But something at her back stopped her.

Will slipped his hand from her death grip and slid it around her waist. His large, warm hand rested just off the center at the small of her back. It felt like an anchor. She was halfway into his embrace. All she needed to do was turn slightly, and she'd find herself fully in his embrace.

Tricksy turned, and she felt herself lock into place at the center of Will Matthews's chest. She looked up. Will smiled down at her.

He hadn't balked at her lie. He hadn't even twitched a brow. He truly was the most decent man she knew, and she was using him. Again.

Only a couple of hours ago, she'd pledged to be a better friend to him. To not use his shoulder as a tissue. Yet here she was again, physically leaning on him when her feelings were hurt.

As cake was being passed around, Tricksy gave Will a tug. He came willingly, though his gaze lingered for a quick second on the iced cake. They headed out onto the porch, out of earshot of everyone in the house.

The kids' glee at having cake in the afternoon could still be heard. So could the horses chomping down on their hay. The chickens Father Matthews kept treated the noonday sun like it was the early morning sun and the roosters crowed.

"I'm so sorry, Will. I don't know what came over me."

Will said nothing. He just lifted his head to the sky. The rays warmed his sun kissed face. The angles were sharp as the sun cast shadows under his eyes and beneath his chin.

"It's just that Foxy was talking about being together in the wedding, being a group again, and something in my head just snapped."

"You miss your sisters."

"I doh..." That lie wouldn't roll so easily off her tongue. "I'll tell them the truth."

Will said nothing. Only turned that piercing gaze on her. The rays of the sun softened as he looked down at her, chasing the shadows away.

"It won't be the first time Foxy got a prediction wrong," Tricksy said.

"She didn't get it wrong."

Now it was Tricksy who went quiet. The sun slipped from Will and shone its rays on her. She felt heat at her back, between her shoulder blades. She felt warmth between her brows.

"I have feelings for your, Tricks."

"Feelings?" She felt sweat in her palms, followed by an instant cooling.

"Beyond friendly ones. Far past sibling feelings." Will lifted his hand to just above his head. "They're right up against the border of love."

Part of Tricksy's brain itched for a pen and paper to write down the poetic words. It was her heart that was racing too fast to allow her to move.

Was she making this up? Was she hearing things? Topher had said lovely words to her before, and he'd never lived up to a single one.

Her fool heart should take a chill pill. But this was Will it was racing for. Will, who was kind and compassionate and had those kissable lips that she had just started to notice.

"You love me?" Tricksy asked.

Will inhaled slowly, deeply.

Tricksy felt the breath leave her body as she waited for his response. What did she want it to be? Did she want Will to love her? Did she love Will?

Of course, she didn't love Will. She loved Topher. Didn't she?

"Listen," he said finally. "You've already told them that we're together. So why don't we try it out?"

"Try out being together?"

"Well, marriage might be a little too soon." Will shrugged, his good-natured grin firmly in place.

That good-natured grin that featured his pillow soft lips. If they tried out being together, Tricksy could get the chance to kiss those lips. But what happened after the kiss?

After a few kisses and Topher had called it quits. He'd gone on to kiss other girls and Tricksy hadn't been kissed again. Instead, she'd written angry lyrics about a broken heart.

"I'd like to take your out for a romantic dinner, or a picnic in the woods, or a horseback ride on the trails. Just the two of us. We can talk and spend time alone and see if you might develop feelings for me that are stronger than friendly or sibling-ly."

Will's hand reached up to brush her temple. The

sweat that had started to pool there cooled. Her shoulders relaxed as she leaned into his touch. She was meant to be answering his question, but all she could do was watch his lips. She wanted him to say more beautiful words to her.

She had been tricked by a man's beautiful words before. But this was Will. Will had always been decent and kind. If Will kissed her, he wouldn't call it quits soon after to go off kissing other girls. Because Will Matthews was the exact opposite of his brother.

Tricksy tilted her head up. Will's nostrils flared as he gazed down at her lips. She would answer him. She would give her answer just as soon as she tasted his lips to know for sure.

Will leaned down. Tricksy went up on her tiptoes. And then-

"Excuse us."

They sprang apart as Charlie and Joe darkened the porch door.

CHAPTER ELEVEN

*S*iblings were the worse. Will hadn't known that in his early days, having been born an only child. When he'd been brought to America and later placed into the foster care system, he'd had an adjustment to the noise of all the other kids. There was often a lot of silence and discipline in North Korea. There had never been a moment of quiet at the Bright Horizons Foster Home. Even less so in the Matthews's house.

His five brothers joyed in playing pranks while others were sleeping. But they never managed to wake Will from his silent nightmares. Not the ever present feeling of hunger pains that felt all too real in his dreams. Not the teeth clenching need to be silent less the government think your traitorous.

Will's parents had been traitors. They had both wanted to defect. When his father had had the chance, his mother had shoved Will into his arms. As the two males had gotten across the border, they learned his mother had been killed for their efforts.

Along with his parents and siblings. That was the way of the country. If one person rebelled, anyone connected with that person was killed.

So Will had learned it was best to stay silent, even when the nightmares came. Even when the dreams were good ones. Will's boyhood dreams had always been about Tricksy James. The girl with the big voice who wasn't afraid to use it.

Will wasn't even sleeping right now. He had Tricksy in his arms. He had everything in his life he'd ever wanted. He was about to have his first taste of his dream. So, of course, his brothers had to show up and ruin it all.

"Excuse me," Tricksy said before stepping down the porch and heading towards the horses.

It took everything in Will to let her go. He'd finally done it. He'd told her how he felt, and she hadn't laughed at him. She hadn't looked at him with pity.

Her nostrils had flared. A spark of curiosity had lit in those dark eyes of hers. Her gaze had landed on his mouth, as though she'd wanted to kiss him. He'd nearly kissed Tricksy James until his two nightmares of brothers ruined it.

Will wanted to turn to his brothers and curse them out using the foulest language he knew; and he knew a lot, having been raised in a state home and later around hardened soldiers. But he knew anger served no purpose other than to hurt the ones he loved. Besides, he couldn't take his gaze off Tricksy.

He'd finally told her how he felt. She hadn't run screaming. She hadn't shot him down. She'd seemed surprised… and interested. He knew he could've won her over if only he'd stolen that kiss.

"So, we're stealing our brother's girlfriends now, are we?"

Will rounded on Charlie, his fists clenched. "Tricksy and Topher were together for a few weeks years ago. Practically a decade."

Charlie's mouth fell slack. Will knew why. It was a rare occurrence indeed to hear Will raise his voice, or his fist.

Though his fists weren't raised. Just clenched. Still, it was more anger than anyone had seen from him in all his years at Flying Cross combined.

"Still," said Joe. "It's bro-code. You're breaking bro-code. Thou shalt not date his brother's ex."

"Fine." Will unclenched his fists and opened his palms towards his brother. "Show me the law book where that's written."

Joe and Charlie shared a look. The slack left Charlie's face and was replaced by a look of sheer mischief. Joe's brows lowered, like a gavel hammering out a final decree of judgement.

Will didn't have time for his brother's shenanigans. He turned back to the fields. But Tricksy was nowhere to be seen.

For a second, he panicked. Had she slipped through his fingers just when he'd gotten ahold of her?

Then he saw the door to the guest house swaying a bit. That's where the girls always stayed when they came to visit when they were younger, and that time after their mother had passed. That was likely where Savy and Foxy were staying until Charlie and Joe put rings on their fingers and said their vows before their father and God -in that order. So that was likely where Tricksy must have gone.

"Besides, Topher was never in love with her," said Will. "He was only into the notion that she had a crush on him."

Both before and after Tricksy, Topher had never had a serious girlfriend. Topher had never had a girlfriend, period. There were tons of girls. Some of them friends. But the only one who had ever gotten that combined label, even if for a brief period, had been Tricksy.

"Are you sure that's all it was for Tricksy?" asked Charlie. "It looked to me like she was in love."

That called Will up short. Tricksy had believed she was important to Topher. The relationship had meant more to her than it ever had to Topher.

"That was my fault." Will had told Tricksy his feelings, but he hadn't told her the whole truth. Now was a good time to practice. "I told Topher what to say to her."

He'd expected surprise on his brothers' faces. Or at least censure. The two men shared a look that was a mix of disappointment and under-standing.

"It was what I was feeling," Will went on. "I just wanted her to be happy."

"You Cyrano de Bergerac'd her?" said Joe. "Bro, that's even worse."

And now, Will couldn't make any eye contact with either of them. His gains of only moments ago felt cheapened. "What was I supposed to do? She only ever looked at me like I was her buddy."

Charlie came over and clapped him on the back.

His large hand gave Will a brotherly squeeze. "But you guys got that out in the open now, right?"

Will winced.

Charlie loosened his grip on Will's shoulder and dropped his hand.

Joe's brows came down again, the judgement even heavier this time.

"You don't want to start off a relationship with a lie," said Charlie, sounding very much like their father.

Again, Will couldn't hide his wince.

Joe raised his finger as though he was in court making an objection. "You are in a real relationship with her? Or was that just to show her sisters up? I know Tricksy and Sav have a weird competition thing going on."

"I told her how I felt," said Will. "Now I just have to hope I can convince her to feel the same way."

"How are you going to do that?"

"Same way I helped Topher win her heart. I'm going to romance her with my words. Only this time, it's going to come straight from me."

CHAPTER TWELVE

 ricksy had stayed in the Flying Cross Ranch guest house a few times in her life. Namely, right after her mother had passed away from a drug overdose. Mrs. Matthews had taken the girls in after they'd heard the news and for a few days after the funeral.

It had been a handful of days filled with warm food, clean sheets, and caring hugs whenever the girls wanted. Most of the time, they didn't have to ask. Even all six of the Matthews boys were kind and careful with them. Charlie never let go of Savy's hand. Joe had dogged Foxy's steps. Topher hadn't hung close to Tricksy, but that had never been his way.

He'd given her a few niceties like *sorry for your*

loss, but not how are you holding up. Then he'd disappeared into the bunkhouse, a place the girls weren't allowed. She hadn't seen much of him after that, but she had seen Will.

Will had asked after her feelings. Will had asked what she needed. Will had sat quietly by her, offering his shoulder. All the while, Tricksy's eyes had never strayed from the bunkhouse, hoping for a sighting of Topher.

Tricksy could see the bunkhouse from the guest-house's window. It had been painted a different color since her time here. She saw the two little girls, LaTisha and Daria, coming out of the doorway of the now coed space. The girls grinned at each other and broke into a run. Looking for all the world like two wild and carefree children who were exactly where they belonged.

The Jameses had all had hopes of an adoption when they were that age, but their mother would never let them go completely. She'd always kept herself just well enough to look like she was trying for rehabilitation. As soon as the authorities' backs were turned, she'd put a needle in her arm. By the time she'd passed on, Savy was a legal adult and Tricksy wasn't too far behind. The door on their opportunity to become a Matthews had closed.

Then they'd lost Mrs. Matthews. Tessa Matthews's death had been a far bigger blow than their own mother's had. Because, despite not being able to take the girls on as her own, Mrs. Matthews had shown up for them time and again because she actually cared about the girls. When Tricksy wondered if someone might be proud of her accomplishments, it was always Mrs. Matthews's face in her mind.

"So, you and Will?"

Tricksy didn't turn at the sound of her sister's voice. She kept her gaze on LaTisha and Daria as they ran towards the end of the drive. In the distance, a school bus ambled its way down the road. The silence in the guesthouse was so loud that Tricksy heard the giggles of the girls outside clearly. Finally, she turned and faced the silent inquisitor.

Savy stood with her arms crossed over her chest. She was decked out in a pair of jeans that fit her curvy form to a T. Tricksy's lower lip twitched to hold shut. She desperately wanted to ask to borrow the denim, knowing that if they fit Savy, then they'd fit like a glove on her.

Tricksy remained quiet.

So did Savy.

It was a power play. One Tricksy knew she'd

lose. As a singer, Tricksy couldn't abide silence for too long.

"Will's a good guy," she said, breaking the stalemate.

"I know," said Savy.

"You know?" Tricksy crossed her arms over her chest, affecting the same stance as her sister. "Let me guess, since you know Will's a good guy, you're wondering what he's doing with the likes of me."

Savy's hands moved to her hips. "I didn't say that."

"You didn't have to." Tricksy mirrored the movement. Then, when she saw that she was in the exact same pose as her big sister, she clasped her hands behind her back. "You always judge me."

"I have never judged you." Savy raised a finger as though it was a point of order. "Except when you're off key."

Tricksy's hands shot from behind her back and punched downward to the floor. For good measure, since her hands didn't make a sound, she stomped her foot. "I have never sung off key a day in my life. Except that time when you decided to change the key of that Whitney Houston song."

"Don't blame me cause you don't have the range."

Savy waved her hand in the air as though she were brushing notes off an imaginary musical scale.

The sound of disbelief that escaped Tricksy's throat hit the range in question. "I don't have the range? You don't-"

"Guys!"

The two sisters turned to see their baby sister in the door of the guesthouse. Clouds moved into sight in the blue sky behind Foxy, threatening a storm on what had been shaping up to be a perfect sunny day.

"If your voices get any louder, you'll scare the horses," said Foxy.

Savy affected a look of innocence. It was a look Tricksy had seen many a time in their youth. It was a look that told Tricksy that Savy knew that she was in the wrong, but she would deny it if an authority figure asked.

Foxy wasn't exactly an authority figure, but she was often the buffer between her two big-voiced siblings. It was often Foxy, the psychic in the family, who was the voice of reason during Savy and Tricksy's arguments. Instead of launching into a lecture, Foxy opened her arms to Tricksy.

"You're home!"

Tricksy allowed herself to be swallowed up by

her baby sister's embrace. It felt good. Foxy smelled the same. She felt the same. But different.

Tricksy knew why. "You're getting married," she squealed.

"I'm getting married," Foxy squealed back. "And so are you."

The squeal died on Tricksy's lips. Her heart thudded with excitement at the thought of getting married. It was something she had always wanted; a man to sweep her off her feet after going down on one knee. She'd dreamed that man was Topher when she was younger. But now her dream man wasn't a brooding blond. The man of her dreams was slowly morphing into a dark-haired man with a heart-shaped smile.

"I knew it," Foxy was saying. "I saw it happening in one of my visions. Will was sitting in the dark, watching you in the light. Each vision, he got closer and closer."

That dream sounded creepy and not at all like Will. But Tricksy had learned it was better to smile and nod when Foxy relayed one of her visions.

"Will moved in sooner than I had expected. You two are ahead of schedule. But that's great. Now we can all get married at the same time."

"Foxy, that's a bit premature," said Savy.

"What are you saying?" Tricksy turned a glare on her oldest sister. "That I'm not good enough to be a part of your wedding?"

"I didn't say that." Savy held up both her hands. "I just figured you weren't at the same stage as the two of us."

Tricksy grit her teeth at the word *stage.* No, she wasn't on the same stage as her sisters. They'd gotten off the stage. Tricksy was the last woman standing, the last woman singing.

"How long have you and Will been dating, anyway?"

"Not long," Tricksy begrudgingly admitted. "But we've been friends forever. And he told me he's had feelings for me for a long time. I'm just catching up now."

It was the truth. It was all the truth. Her heart was racing even now. But the question was, could it catch up to Will's?

CHAPTER THIRTEEN

Will grabbed fresh fruit from the fridge. He knew that Tricksy had a thing for apples. Her favorite movie as a kid was *Snow White and the Seven Dwarves*. She had fixated on the apple that the old hag had given Snow White. True, it had poisoned the princess and put her into a sleep, but that sleep had given her her prince. Therefore Tricksy found it romantic.

Will tested two apples, making sure they were firm, which meant they would be sweeter. He placed those into the picnic basket. Satisfied with his wares, he closed the fridge and turned around.

A sound coming from the closet pulled him up short. The sound was too large to be a rodent, and not a single rodent had ever dared come into Tessa

Matthews's house. The boys were sure her ghost came in the night to dust away the cobwebs and tidy up the corners.

A second sound came from the closet. It was a definite squeak. But not a vocal squeak that would come from a tiny throat. More like the squeak of a pair of sneakers against the floor.

Since it was a Monday morning and all the kids were off to school, Will could hazard a guess what, or rather who, the culprit was. He pulled open the closet door and his suspicions were confirmed.

"Nothin' here to see. So why don't you just let me be?"

Will winced at the kid's bad rhyme. He'd been treated to it all last night during dinner whenever Ashton, who would only answer to the nickname Ashtray, spoke.

As a quiet kid who preferred books to people, the closet had been one of Will's favorite hiding places as a kid. There were a number of times he'd been in there and had forgotten to make it to the school bus. Since there was no book in his hands, Will was fairly certain Ashtray had missed the school bus on purpose.

"Did you find what you were looking for in there? A dust pan? Broom?"

Ashtray looked around the small place as though he was just now realizing it was a broom closet filled with cleaning supplies.

"I assume since you decided to stay home from school, and that you're in the broom closet, you're going to help my father and Charlie with the day's chores?"

The gulp down the kid's narrow throat and into his small chest was audible. "Uh, yeah, yo. I'm about to clean up, bro. That's why I'm behind this doh."

Will had read and heard some truly bad poetry in his days, but this kid? Oh, this kid's verses were brutal. Ashtray stepped out of the closet and into the light. That's when Will saw another sign of brutality.

Beneath Ashtray's shirt collar, between his neck and his shoulder, was the unmistakable outline of a handprint. It looked as though someone had grabbed him there, very roughly. The handprint was smaller than Will's, but slightly bigger than Ashtray's hands.

"You having some trouble at school, Ash?"

The kid pursed his lips. Whether in preparation for another ill-constructed rhyme, or a stalling tactic to determine what lie he could tell, Will wasn't sure. He knew he wouldn't get the truth from this kid who had known him for less than a day. If Will wanted to be trusted, he'd have to give some of his own first.

"It was hard for me when I first came to this country. I didn't speak the language, and I looked different from everyone else."

Ash swiped a blond braid from his startlingly blue eyes.

"I got picked on a lot."

Ash's eyes lit up at that. "But you hit them with that kung fu. Made them do what they do."

"I'm Korean, not Chinese."

Confusion darkened the kid's gaze. He clearly didn't know much about the differences in culture. Especially not when he was affecting an urban accent. An accent that vacillated from the sunny West coast, and other times to inner cities of the East. The kid meshed up the slang from Snoop Dog to Puff Daddy, which made his speech pattern all the more messy.

"Things got better for me when I learned English, and I began to use my words. You see, no one could understand me at first. Once I could speak to them, using my own words, we saw that we had a lot in common."

The we in question were his brothers. Topher and the twins, Mateo and Aldo, had been Will's first bullies when he came to live at Bright Horizons. They pushed and shoved and stole his food. They played pranks and made him miserable.

Once he learned English, he was able to tell them to stop. No, Topher didn't listen to his plea at first. Instead, he'd laughed at Will's garbled accent. But that was only at first.

The more words Will learned, the more words he used. The more words he hurled at Topher, the more Topher began to listen. Until the two saw that they had a lot in common. Pretty soon, Topher didn't stop talking to Will. Then, if anyone else dared push, shove, or steal from Will, it was Topher who stepped up to Will's side.

"You clearly have a lot to say, Ash. But I think it might be hard for other kids to understand your rhymes when they're still learning proper English themselves. Maybe if you spoke more plainly, you'd have a little better understanding?"

The kid pursed his lips again. He scratched at his side, where his pants hung low on his skinny frame. "You not gonna rat me out to Ms. Savy?"

There was no rhyming in that sentence, so Will felt he'd been heard. "I think if you get on with those chores, she might not be so mad."

Savy loved chores. If the kid got a few done

before she found him, he wouldn't come away with too big a punishment for missing a day of school. Maybe?

But when Ash grabbed the mop and headed out the backdoor, Will wasn't so sure it was going to work out for him. He couldn't deal with that drama anymore. He had a more pressing arrangement to get to. When he turned around, he came face to face with his father.

"Hey, Dad."

"Son," his father nodded at him, an easy smile on his face.

It was rare to find Haran Matthews frowning. Even with a house full of rambunctious, mostly feral boys. That smile was a loaded weapon. If it even began to turn downward, the Matthews boys would hop into formation to complete whatever chore or correct whatever wrong that had displeased their father.

"I helped with chores this morning already," said Will. "I was just headed out for lunch."

"With Tricksy."

Will Matthews wasn't one to blush, but he felt his cheeks heat. "I love her, Dad. Always have. I finally got the courage to tell her so."

"I know you were in love with her. Never understood why you stepped aside for your brother." Haran Matthews looked him up and down. "Though, no, maybe I do understand."

Will waited for Father Matthews to explain his meaning. When the silence stretched on for a couple of seconds, he knew it wasn't coming. His father was not a fan of spoon feeding his boys the answers to questions. In grade school, he frowned at calculators, preferring to have the boys do long division and algebra on scrap paper. Said it built character.

So whatever Father Matthews thought Will had to learn about making way for Topher to sweep the woman he loved off her feet, he would have to wait until Will completed every step of the problem. But that was fine. Because Will wasn't going to make the same mistake in coming to a solution to this.

"I got some mail for you," said Father Matthews.

He handed Will an envelope. Will cringed when he saw the From address. It was from the FAA, the Federal Aviation Administration.

This was not how he wanted to tell his father about his decision to stop flying. Will's decision to start in the commercial flight business instead of joining the Air Force, or even the reserves, had been a slap in his father's face. Though the old man had never said so. But Will still knew.

"Congratulations, son," said Father Matthews.

Will blinked a few times. Had he heard his father correctly? Was the old man being sarcastic? That wasn't his way.

Father Matthews handed his son another package. This one was opened. "I'm sorry that I opened it. I couldn't figure out who it was addressed to with only the initials and I thought the contents would give me a clue."

Inside the opened envelope was the proof of a book. A book of poetry. The author was J. Matthews.

"How'd you figure this was by me?" he asked his father.

"Aside from knowing my son's true name," Father Matthews grinned, "which other of my sons has a gift for the written word?"

Will's Korean name was Ji-Hoon. When he'd come to America, the case worker had trouble saying it and began calling him William.

Father Matthews didn't ask Will why he hadn't published the book in his family name. But he didn't have to. Will had found the courage to tell the woman he loved about his feelings, but he still wasn't ready to tell his family about his other passion.

"I'm proud of you." Haran Matthews opened his arms. Will came obligingly. But he wasn't certain he'd heard his father right.

"You said you're proud? Not mad?"

"What would I have to be mad about?"

"I quit flying to become a poet."

"Ah," Father Matthews nodded. "So you're telling me you finally stopped doing what you thought I wanted you to do and you're doing what's in your heart?"

"Um… well, yes."

"Words have always been your greatest strength, son. I'm happy you're taking the credit for them instead of hiding them away in notebooks or giving them to your brother to use for his purposes."

There was a twinkle in his father's eyes as he said the words. Will felt like that was a part of the lesson he was supposed to learn. Well, after years of long division with no calculator, he'd finally come to the solution. He'd told Tricksy how he felt and now he was headed out to spend the afternoon with the answer to all his heart's desires.

CHAPTER FOURTEEN

The sun played peekaboo with the clouds. The clouds were white, fluffy affairs, so Tricksy doubted it would rain. Despite the turbulent morning, the day was far too perfect for a storm.

She'd had a good breakfast with her sisters. Foxy had gabbed during most of it, trying to fill Tricksy in on a year's worth of town gossip. Savy had kept casting Tricksy sidelong glances, but she hadn't said too much. The two of them had come to a truce of sorts. Though Tricksy was certain she was doing far more to keep the peace than her older sister.

There were only two clean forks in the guest house. Instead of insisting that the actual guest in the house get the utensil, Tricksy ate her eggs with a spoon. Savy and Foxy were headed out to do chores, whereas Tricksy had a date. But Tricksy waited patiently for twenty minutes while Savy did her hair, which would easily come down under the noonday sun and the chores she had planned.

When Tricksy emerged from the bathroom and headed for the path behind the house instead of the barn, Savy had sucked her teeth. It was evident her older sister wanted Tricksy to participate in the chores. But she was going on a date and she was wearing a sundress.

Yet did Tricksy put up an argument? Nope. She smiled sweetly and turned on her heel to take Will's arm. Luckily, her back was to Savy as her smirk spread across her face.

Tricksy felt like a princess as she walked arm and arm with Will. He led her into the forest, near a small pond that was bordered by the Flying Cross Ranch and the Silver Star Ranch. The spot was idyllic, romantic, like something out of a Disney movie. She expected bluebirds to land on a branch and serenade them.

Unfortunately, that didn't happen. The lack of cartoon avians didn't detract from the magic of the day. She and Will had had many a meal together when they were younger. But the air was different this time.

Tricksy stepped off the path and her heel instantly stuck into the rich earth. Will gave her a tug, and she came into his arms. Their lips were just a few inches away from each other. It was the perfect moment for a kiss.

They both pulled back.

Will took her hand again. He lead her on a sturdy part of the path, pointing out places to avoid stepping in her impractical shoes. She knew the shoes were impractical. But she'd wanted to make herself pretty for Will.

After Will laid out a blanket, he held out his hand to help her into a seated position. No man had ever done that before and Tricksy was charmed. When Will joined her on the blanket, they gazed at each other shyly. Their smiles were wide, but neither of them spoke. Tricksy tugged at the bottom of her lower lip. Will tugged his upper lip into his mouth. When he caught her staring, she turned away.

A giggle escaped her lips and Will looked over at her.

"Is this insane?" she asked.

"What?"

"Us?"

He blinked.

"Not insane like crazy, or bad. Just insane, like

unexpected? Not that I was expecting it? I just... Why am I all of a sudden tongue tied around you? We've always been good at talking to each other."

"Maybe because now you know how much I want to kiss you?"

The breath left her in a whoosh. Will had never spoken to her like this in all their years of knowing each other. He'd never looked at her like he was now. There was heat in his gaze, but he held himself back.

Suddenly, Tricksy wanted to kiss his lips more than anything in the world. It wasn't her belly that was grumbling. It was something in her throat, a dark desire that wanted to be addressed.

"But you didn't," she said. "Just then, when I fell into your arms. You… didn't."

"No. I didn't."

"That kind of makes me question just how much you want to do it, then."

She was goading him, and she knew it. She wasn't determined not to be the kind of girl who chased men. She wanted to be chased. She wanted him to make the first move.

"I will," he said.

"When?"

"When I've earned it."

Tricksy wanted to argue more, but she decided to hush. Will had declared his feelings, but he wasn't pushing her. He was chasing her, but allowing her to be just beyond his reach. In truth, it was a bit thrilling.

Will reached over to open the basket. Out of its belly, he pulled sliced apples and buttery croissants.

"My favorite," she said.

Will nodded. He arranged the treats for her on a plate. He picked up the neatly arranged dish and presented it to her. When Tricksy's hand met Will's, a spark of electricity zapped her fingers. She knew he felt it too, by the flare of his nostrils.

A bird cawed in the tree above, further adding to the Disney-like feeling of the scene. In the midst of the song, the bird promptly did its business. The little gift landed at the center of her plate.

Tricksy glared up at the bird for ruining her perfect moment.

Will chuckled and put the plate aside. He pulled a single slice of apple from the basket and held it out for her. Instead of taking it in her hand, Tricksy leaned forward, parting her lips.

Will stared for a moment, his features dumbfounded. Then he got himself together and raised the morsel to her mouth.

Tricksy crunched down on the apple. It wasn't the sexiest sound. Nor was it the most elegant food to eat when trying to flirt with the guy you're dating. But the fruit was sweet and the guy who gave it to her was just as sweet.

Will fed her another apple slice. Followed by a torn piece of croissant. Each bite was better than the last. Likely because they had been carefully selected and were now being presented to her by a man who truly cared for her.

"Thank you for this, Will," she said.

"It's my pleasure." He smiled, his gaze on her lips as she swallowed down the last bite.

Tricksy wasn't going to play coy anymore. She wasn't going to wait for Will to think he deserved her. She reached for him and pulled him down to her lips for a searing kiss.

Fireworks went off behind her eyes. Her heart pumped out an erratic series of beats. It had been so long that the organ had been broken that it didn't realize it was skipping beats.

When they pulled apart, Will looked at her. His dark gaze appeared just as dazed as she felt. "We probably shouldn't get married."

"What?"

"Next week, with our brothers and sisters."

Now it was Tricksy who blinked. She wanted to cup her hand to her mouth and breathe into her palm. Perhaps she'd bitten into a bad apple and the smell was on her breath?

"I don't want to rush this," Will was saying. "There's so much we need to learn about each other. And I want to do this right. I want you to see that I'm the man for you. And there are things I haven't told you."

"What things?"

He hesitated. He opened his mouth, and that's when the sky decided to pour out its heart.

Will clutched her to him as the rain poured down. He stood with her in his arms and used the picnic blanket to shelter her. It didn't matter that she was getting soaked through. It didn't matter what he wanted to tell her that he hadn't. Tricksy knew that this man would never hurt her and that let her know that she was safe with him and they'd weather any storm.

CHAPTER FIFTEEN

Will held his hand out flat. The apple contained in his palm was snagged quickly by the mare. Duff had been his favorite when he arrived on the ranch. The stallion had always been the gentlest of horses, never showing any signs of temper. He was getting on in years now. So Will snuck him a second apple.

His good deed done for the day, he turned. Only to find that the gate was open. A new to him stallion was out and about. The young buck grazed in the open pastures. Having a horse outside of the pen with no one attending him could be a danger. It would be best if the horse was back in the pen with the gate closed firmly behind him.

Will approached the horse with slow steps. The

horse raised his head and eyed Will warily. Will took in his options to get the horse back in the pen.

He knew he had to watch the pressure he put the horse under as he systematically cut off options for escape. He could run the horse until the beast tired itself out. But he only wanted the animal to move as much as necessary, and only in the direction he wanted. Anything that would hurt the horse was out of bounds. His father wouldn't abide any kind of animal cruelty.

Will kept his demeanor calm. He didn't want to give off any negative vibes or do anything that would cause the horse to aggress. He grabbed a coiled lariat, not a lunge whip. His father had taught him to use the lariat as an extension of his arm to get the horse to follow his commands.

Horses were extremely intelligent creatures, but also empathetic. Will focused his gaze on the horse's hip. He made a kissing sound with his lips. Then he motioned with his hand. The horse took a step forward. Will relaxed his stance even more, letting the lariat hang loosely. It appeared the two understood one another.

Will made another sound and another hand motion. The horse took a few more tentative steps. Will nodded his head, speaking soothingly to the animal. Within a minute, the horse was back inside the gate. Will hadn't had to raise his voice or the lariat.

He did wonder at who would've left a gate open on the ranch. It couldn't have been one of his brothers. They'd had it drilled in the head that you always close a gate behind you on a ranch or an animal would get out. Or get in, which could be even worse.

It had to be one of the foster kids. But they were all at school today. Except Will saw a pair of sneakers peeking out of one of the stalls in the barn.

Once again, Will approached the animal with caution. He placed the lariat on a hook on the wall. At the stall, he leaned over slowly and looked down.

"Ashton?"

"No," said the kid. "It's Ashtray."

"Right. My mistake. Do you mind if I call you Ash? Ashtray is a place where you discard something you no longer want. I don't think that represents you."

The kid stared at the ground. With the toe of his shoes, he kicked up some of the dirt. Then, when a few specks got on his shoes, he balanced on one foot to rub the dirt off onto his low hanging jeans.

"Did you miss the school bus again, Ash?"

He looked up now. His eyes were red, as though

he'd been crying. Will averted his gaze and stared at the wall. The last thing a little boy wanted an adult male to know was that he'd been crying.

"I'm taking the day off. I need a self-care day."

"Self care day?"

"Yeah, Ms. Foxy takes them all the time."

"Ms. Foxy is a grown woman." Though that was debatable sometimes with the antics her visions had her get up to. "You haven't earned that right yet."

"Please. I can't deal with him today. I'll go back tomorrow."

Will opened the door to the stall slowly. He made his movements small, just like he'd done with the horse. He came inside and crouched down next to Ash until they were at eye level. "Somebody giving you trouble?"

"I'm handling it."

Will nodded, remaining mute. In his experience, if he waited patiently, the other person would always fill the silence.

"I tried being myself. But he doesn't like who I am, so he grabbed me by the neck and shoved me and ruined my pants. I had to hide it from Ms. Savy because she would go down to the school and call his teachers and his parents and probably the mayor, too. Then I would never have any street cred."

That sounded like Savy.

"I can't tell Mr. Charlie because he'll tell Ms. Savy. And I've been avoiding Ms. Foxy because I don't want her to see what's been going on with her psychic powers, because she'll tell Ms. Savy."

Ash ended his diatribe in a rush, with his small chest caving in. He must have been holding that in for so long that letting out had emptied him out. He leaned his head against Will's shoulder, a few of his braids unraveling as he did so.

"What do you think I should do, Mr. Will?"

"Me?"

The kid nodded.

"I think that every bully needs a victim. They need someone else to bully so that someone won't bully them."

"So, you think I should find the bully's bully and talk to them?"

"No, I think you should stay out of his path. Don't give him a chance to make you a victim."

"So, in other words, run and hide."

"That's not what-"

"So, I can stay home today and have a self care day?"

Will sighed. He'd been had, again. If he kept this up, Savy would have his hide. "All right. But you're helping me with chores. And you have to make sure you close doors behind you from now on."

"Deal," he said, headed out the stall door, leaving it flapping open behind him as he raced out into the fields.

CHAPTER SIXTEEN

Tricksy twisted her hair up into two pin curls. Looping the curls around the curling iron, she tamed her thick, dark hair into what looked like a series of waves that a surfer would love to ride. A few of the tendrils she left to hang down her long neck, hoping to draw attention there during the evening's festivities.

The thought of Will's gaze on her neck brought a flush to her cheeks. The thought of his lips brushing the bottom tendril of her hair spread that blush all across her neck.

A third tendril escaped the pinned up curls atop her head, likely eager to join the party at the bottom. Tricksy reached for her hairspray, only to realize she'd left it in the other bathroom back at the guest house.

She'd been trying to get into the guest house bathroom for two hours. With her two sisters also trying to get ready, she'd had to resort to coming into the big house to do her hair. If she tried to trek back across the yard to the guesthouse, more curls would likely riot and join the party around her neck. The only thing to do was to attack them with more pins to keep them in their place.

By the time Tricksy had stopped the rebellion in its tracks, and she was developing a migraine, there was a knock on the door.

"It's occupied."

The person on the other side rattled the locked doorknob. Tricksy turned, exasperated. She was certain it was Savy.

She pulled the door open and was immediately pressed back inside the room. A tall form loomed over her. Strong, muscled arms came around her. Lips in the shape of a heart captured her mouth.

Tricksy surrendered to the intruder without a sound. No, that wasn't true. A moan of pure delight escaped her lips when they parted as Will deepened the kiss.

Will's kiss was so gentle that it forced Tricksy to cling to him violently. Her back was pressed up against the door. The pins in her hair poked into her scalp. But Tricksy wouldn't stop Will's kiss to pull them out. Not for all the hairspray in the world. Not when the softest lips imaginable crashed down upon hers again and again like a tidal wave. She was going to drown, and it was going to be such a good death.

"You're gonna get us in trouble," Tricksy said when she could catch her breath. "Isn't this against your father's rules?"

"Worth it," Will grinned.

He brushed his index finger against the baby hairs on her forehead. He traced his finger down her ear tip. He took one of the tendrils she'd allowed to hang at her neck between his thumb and index finger. The loop of hair curled around Will's finger like a cat tucking in for a belly rub.

"You look beautiful," he said.

"I haven't even put on my makeup."

Will shrugged and pressed a kiss to her temple. It was the most intimate moment of her life, feeling this man with such strength in him handle her so gently. Tricksy felt his nostrils flare and ruffle the hairs atop her head. She felt his inhale and was certain parts of her soul left her body to settle inside this man.

This man was Will, her childhood friend. The shoulder she cried on whenever anything didn't go as she planned. That shoulder beckoned her now. Tricksy rested her head against his shoulder and found the safe space that had always been available to her. Now that place felt more like a warmth hearth that offered comfort, but also sparked with embers that waited to ignite something more.

Tricksy turned her head, tucking her forehead beneath his chin, she rested her hands against his heart. She felt it thumping against her fingertips. Will turned and pressed another gentle kiss to her temple. Tricksy felt a shudder flit across her shoulders and run down her spine until it reached her toes.

She was so full of feelings, so full of emotions, that she didn't quite know what to do with herself. She itched for a pen and paper to write it all down in verse. But she didn't have a clue where to begin.

With her other songs, Tricksy would begin in a lower key. Recounting all the ways, the guy, namely Topher, had done her wrong. Then her voice would rise to its sopranic glory in the chorus as she let her anger and rage have at it.

Standing in the tender embrace of Will Matthews, Tricksy didn't want to start low. Not when she was so high. Could she start a song in a high C? She wasn't sure? She'd never written a song of about happiness.

Because that's what this feeling was. Happy. Secure. Love.

Will had said he loved her. No man had ever said that to her. And Will never lied, so she knew it was true.

The question was not could she write a song about him. The question was, could she love him?

Tricksy looked up at Will. Will gazed down at her. He didn't make any demands. He asked nothing of her but a chance. A chance to let him love her.

"Thank you," she said.

"For what?" he toyed with the tendril of hairs at her nape.

Tricksy shook her head, too embarrassed to confess what she was feeling. Anytime she'd told her true feelings in the past, she'd gotten hurt. But this was Will. Will would never hurt her.

"Thank you for being you," she said. "You're beautiful."

He let go of her hair and turned away with a sheepish grin.

"You are." Tricksy captured his strong chin in her palm and turned him back to face her. "I always thought the girl who won your heart would be the luckiest girl in the world. I never imagined it might be me. I wish you had told me sooner how you felt."

Something shifted in his eyes. "I would have." He took a deep breath, and let the air out away from her and towards the door. "But you were in love with my brother."

"I'm not sure that was love. A crush, maybe. It certainly felt like a crush." For years, the image of Topher was always at the forefront of her mind. Now, standing in the loose embrace of his brother, Tricksy was having trouble picturing the details of the man. "Topher said so many romantic things. But he never behaved the way he spoke. It's like he was two different people."

"Yeah," Will sighed again. His features were contorted in pain when he came back to face her. "About that…"

His lips parted. Then quivered as though he was about to form words. Only to jerk apart again at a knock at the bathroom door.

The door opened to reveal Father Matthews standing on the other side. His usually cheery face displayed a displeased frown.

Will and Tricksy broke apart instantly, retreating to the far corners of the small enclosure as if the two grown adults had been caught with their hands in the cookie jar.

ill was living his dream. Thankfully, he was awake while all the goodness of his childhood hopes and yearnings were happening to him. To say that reality was better than his imagination was the understatement of the decade.

He walked down the street of his adopted hometown with his fingers entwined with the girl who had inhabited all of his childhood, pubescent, and adult fantasies. He was certain everyone was looking at them. That everyone envied him. And why wouldn't they?

Tricksy was a picture in her flaring dress and heels. Her hair done up like a pinup girl from the mid-century, though a few extra tendrils had escaped from the updo after their bathroom tryst.

The thought of their time together behind closed doors made Will grip her hand tighter. In his back pocket was the copy of his book of poetry. The plan was to show her the book, let her read his words, and then launch into the truth about what happened when they were kids. But later.

Right now Tricksy's head rested against his shoulder as they walked hand in hand. Her head on his shoulder had been a frequent occurrence in their youth. Normally, there were tears flowing down her eyes. But tonight, they gleamed bright with happiness.

He'd done that. He'd put that sparkle there. And he planned to do everything in his power to keep it there.

Tricksy deserved to be happy. She deserved to write songs that were heartfelt, not heartbroken. Will wanted to be the inspiration for those ballads.

He ached to hear his name on her lips on a high note. He wanted to hear their love story in a chorus sung over and over again as happy couples danced around a room. He never wanted to hear Tricksy James sing another sad song, not while she was on his arm. And Will had plans to keep this woman at his side for the rest of their lives.

"You don't know how much I needed a night out," said Savy. She walked ahead of Will and Tricksy on Charlie's arm, while Joe and Foxy brought up the rear. "Being a mother is hard work. I thought my parenting days were over after raising these two."

Savy chucked her finger over her shoulder in the direction of her younger sisters. Foxy and Joe weren't listening to a thing Savy said. They were in their own little bubble, too busy gazing at each other.

Will turned to gaze at Tricksy, but Tricks was glaring at her older sister. Her lips, which were coated in a deep red gloss, were pinched together as though she was trying to hold words in. It quickly became apparent that she was going to lose that battle.

"You didn't have to raise us that far. I'm only two years younger than you."

"Yeah, but you wet the bed until you were six."

Tricksy's hand was a death grip on Will's. The tension in her body radiated out to him. Then her face morphed from indignation to the kind mischievous grin he remembered seeing on the Old Hag when she offered Snow White that poisoned apple.

"Oh, you're still mad because I had an accident on Mr. Blankie. Charlie, did you know Savy slept with a special blanket until she was twelve?"

Savy's steps faltered, her features scrunched and her nose wrinkled as though she'd just taken a bite out of a bad apple.

Charlie's arm around her waist propelled his fiancée forward. He cast a meaningful glance at Will. The meaning that rung loud and clear in that glance was *I got mine under control. You keep a handle on yours.*

The command in his brother's gaze rankled, but Will knew Charlie was right. They had to keep the temperature amongst the female siblings cool if they all wanted to have a good time tonight. Luckily, Will was excellent at defusing tense situations.

"Is that Castro's Creamery over there?" Will asked. "I haven't had Old Man Castro's ice cream in years."

"Maybe we should go there," said Charlie, jumping on the distraction band wagon.

"What do you say, Joe?"

"Hmm? What?" Joe struggled and lost the battle to tear his gaze away from Foxy.

"But it's karaoke night at the bar," said Savy. "I'm in the mood to sing. What about you ladies?"

Now it was Will that cast Charlie a glance. Though Will's glance was one of uncertainty? Could more sibling squabbling break out if the girls were singing on stage? He wasn't sure? What he did know was that he wanted to hear Tricksy sing.

"What do you think, Tricks? You wanna share your gift with the undeserving people of this town?"

Tricksy smiled up at him and Will felt like he'd hung the moon. All the tension eased from her face. That's what let him know he'd made the right decision. He squeezed her closer as he steered her into the bar.

Once inside the bar, both Savy and Tricksy made a beeline for the sign-up sheet. At least when they came back to the table, they weren't pushing and shoving.

"When are you headed back on the road, Tricks?" asked Charlie.

"Um... I'm not sure."

"You gonna be traveling with our brother here? Is that legal? Can you fly with your significant other on board commercial flights?"

"I think you're thinking about the medical profession," said Joe. "Doctors can't operate on loved ones."

"I'm retired."

All eyes went to Will's. It was Tricksy's surprised gaze that he focused on.

"You didn't tell me that," she said.

"I wanted to tell my dad first."

The surprise melted away and was replaced with acceptance. Just like that, she gave a nod and appeared to move on. Will hoped his next admission to her went just as smoothly.

"So what are you going to do now?" asked Savy. "How will you support my sister when the two of you are married?"

"That's none of your business, Sav," said Tricksy.

"I think it is. You're my little sister."

"I'm a grown woman, and you're not in charge of my livelihood."

"Someone should be."

Tricksy sat forward, her fingertips holding onto the edge of the tabletop. "What's that supposed to mean?"

"Ronny's Dive bar? Not really an upstanding place."

The blood drained from Tricksy's fingertips as they gripped the table. Before she could get a word out, the announcer called Savy to the stage for her song. Savy rose quickly, smiling and waving to the crowd of townsfolk who knew her and her voice.

Will put an arm around Tricksy, trying to urge her body to relax after that tense exchange.

"You not singing tonight, Foxy?" said Charlie.

"Oh no," said Foxy. "There's a storm brewing."

It was a cloudless night outside. Still, something about Foxy's forecast sounded all too right. On the stage, Savy whipped the crowd into a frenzy with her deep-throated rendition of an Adele song. The applause that followed her performance was thunderous.

"Coming next to the stage is another town favorite. Let's give it up for Ms. Tricksy James."

Tricksy gave Will's hand a squeeze before leaving the table. Will couldn't take his eyes off her as she took the stage. So often he'd hidden in the backs of bars to watch her sing. Now he sat front in center. Not only that, her eyes were on him as she sang the Donny Hathaway classic *A Song for You* that had been made popular again in a higher key by Christina Aguilera.

Tricksy's rendition of the love ballad was pitch perfect. Especially the parts of falling in love with a friend in a place with no space or time. With each word belted out, her gaze never left Will's.

His heart thudded so loudly in his chest that he didn't realize that it was the audience applauding at the conclusion of the song. Even Savy joined in in praising her sister. The look on her teary-eyed face was surprisingly close to pride.

When Tricksy let go of the mic, the MC put up his hands to halt her motion.

"Not so fast," he said with a huge grin. "This is not on the schedule, but I know the crowd here would love to hear the song that made you a local celebrity."

The prickles started at Will's back. The song that had made Tricksy James a local celebrity was the song about her breakup with his brother. Not exactly the thing the new guy wanted to hear when he was trying to win the lady's heart.

The crowd, made up of mostly women, started a slow clap, demanding the song. Tricksy cast Will a glance. In that glance, he could tell she was hesitant to acquiesce to the crowd's demands. Was it because of him? Or was it because she no longer wanted to sing that song?

Will hoped it was the latter. He also hoped it was the former. He wanted Tricksy to be over Topher and take into account his feelings. Unfortunately, what either of them wanted would be a moot point as the track began to play.

Trapped on the stage, Tricksy had no choice but

to start singing the lyrics of the song about how his brother broke her heart. But it sounded different as each word left her lips. Usually Tricksy sang this particular song with a pang in her voice.

There was no pang. There was hardly any emotion. She rushed a few of the lyrics, as though she was just trying to get to the end. Near the middle of the song, which called for higher notes, she faltered.

Savy was out of her seat and at the mic beside her sister. She looped an arm around Tricksy's waist and sang into the side of the mic. In her alto voice, Savy managed to hit the note that Tricksy hadn't been able to reach.

The rest of the song they sang at a lower key, somewhere between Tricksy's high soprano and Savy's lower register. The two finished the song in perfect harmony and to the most applause of the night. Before the applause died down, as Savy was taking a bow with her arm still wrapped around Tricksy's waist, Tricksy ducked out of the embrace and ran off the stage.

CHAPTER EIGHTEEN

She had to get off that stage. She had to get out of there. She had to get away from the audience. She had to get away from her sister.

For months, years even, Tricksy had wished her sisters were standing on the stage at her sides. But that performance of Savy's reminded her of what it had been like. Savy had always taken the spotlight. She had always arranged the music to fit her alto voice when Tricksy wanted to go high and riff and trill.

Tonight, when the spotlight had been on her, Savy had brought Tricksy back down to a place she didn't want to be. Singing about her ex, in a key that wasn't for her, in front of the man she had an actual connection with.

Tricksy hadn't even wanted to sing that song. Her heart hadn't been in it. Not when her heart was now entirely focused on Will.

Will was a man who would never do those things to her that she sang about in the song. Will would never say one thing and then do another. Will would never leave her stranded. Will would never break her heart because Will would never lie to her.

Tricksy had not been in love with Topher, she saw that clearly now. It had been a crush. A silly girlhood crush, and she didn't want to sing about him anymore. She wanted to sing about Will. And she wanted to sing about him in her key.

She jumped when a hand landed on her shoulder. Whirling around, she saw Will. She saw the concern on his face. She saw his hand reaching for her. She saw that comfortable-looking space that was his shoulder and she dove for it.

Will's arms came around her. His lips brushed her temple. He said no words, just made reassuring sounds in her ear as he held her tight.

And that's when she knew. Tricksy knew everything would be alright, because she was with Will. Her heart had chosen Will. The choice was so simple, as if it had always been him.

She had spent half her life pining over Topher,

but she'd fallen in love with Will in the space of a heartbeat. And it was the safest place she'd ever found herself.

"What was that all about, Tricksy?" called Savy.

Tricksy did not want a fight. She did not want to face what was on the other side of Will's shoulder. She wanted to stay hidden inside the comfort of Will's chest.

But this fight was long overdue. And so she turned away from Will's chest. She lifted her head from Will's shoulder. She took a step back from Will. She felt the reluctance with which he let her go.

"You always do that," Tricksy said as she came face to face with her sister.

"Always do what?" said Savy. "Come to your rescue?"

"Did I ask you to come to my rescue?"

"No, you didn't because you were choking on that song."

"I didn't choke. I didn't want to sing it. I've completely outgrown it. I've grown past it. I'm in a new relationship now. A good, healthy relationship with someone who cares about me and doesn't try to steal the spotlight from me."

"I think that last part was about the two of you,

and not Will." Foxy said as she leaned over and spoke those words to Savy.

"Thanks, sis, but I didn't need a psychic to tell me that," said Savy.

"Hey," Foxy held up her hands as she stood between her two sisters, "I'm not a part of this fight. And I'm not a psychic. I'm clair-"

"And that's another thing," said Tricksy, her finger pointing at Foxy. "You never choose sides."

"Why would I choose a side?" said Foxy. "You're my sisters. We stand together."

"We never stood together," said Tricksy. "We stood behind her because we were her background singers."

Savy rolled her gaze skyward. "Here we go."

"And she's doing what she's always done now, which is to try and put me in my place."

"How can I be trying to put you in your place when you're the one who left," said Savy.

"You're the one who didn't stay," said Tricksy.

"How about this," said Foxy. "Here's the perfect time for you two to meet in the middle with me. Come on." Foxy opened her arms and made a hand motion, urging her sisters closer.

"Stay out of it, Foxy," both Savy and Tricksy shouted at their sister.

Foxy threw up her hands, lolling her head back and seeking answers from the same sky as Savy. The sky was still void of clouds, but the storm was picking up here on the ground.

"You say you wanted to mother me," Tricksy was saying, "but you left me to go and take care of people who weren't your flesh and blood. You left me alone to deal with the world."

"You wanted to stay on the road," said Savy. "I couldn't stop you from going."

"Yeah, you could've."

"How?"

"You could've told me you wanted me to stay home."

The two sisters stared at each other. Both of their chests heaving as though they'd been running hard and fast and came to an abrupt halt. Their postures both stiff and flinching at the same time.

Tricksy had thought she'd felt relief at having finally had it out with her sister. Instead, a weight settled on her chest. The butterflies that always danced in her belly before and after a performance were silent and huddled in a corner of her gut, uncertain of what the calm in the center of this storm would bring.

"What do we do now?" asked Foxy.

Savy let out a forceful breath, her shoulders heaving downward. "I want to go and have ice cream."

Tricksy let out a weary sigh, her arms coming around her middle. "I want to go home."

Savy turned left and headed with Charlie to the ice cream shop.

Tricksy turned right and headed back to the car with Will.

A glance over her shoulders showed Tricksy that Foxy had stayed where she was in the middle of the sidewalk, head swinging from right to left as she watched her sisters retreat to opposite sides.

CHAPTER NINETEEN

he moon was high over the barn. The ranch was quiet in the cool night. The sky was still cloudless, but Will had just weathered a storm for the ages.

For the second time this week, Will slowed the car to a stop on the ranch. The gravel under the tires was as quiet as the interior of the car. The lights were out in the main house, as well as the guest house and the bunkhouse. Even the bugs halted in their creeping, uncertain if it was safe to make any move.

Will had known things weren't perfect between the James sisters. When were things ever perfect in a family of differing views and temperaments? But he'd never known how wide the rift between Savy and Tricksy actually was.

A few miles back, the anger had dissipated off of Tricksy's face. All that remained on her beautiful features was hurt and sorrow. Will reached out to her. He couldn't help himself, not now when he had finally earned himself the right to touch her.

He placed his thumb at the center of her brow. With gentle pressure, he tried to smooth the worry lines that creased her forehead. What he got for his efforts was a long and weary sigh as Tricksy dipped her head so that the weight of it was cradled in Will's palm.

They stayed like that for long moments. Will brushed his thumb and forefinger idly across her forehead and temples.

"You should talk to her," said Will.

"I don't want to talk to her. She's a bully."

"Well, you know the thing about bullies?"

"They have big mouths and big heads and go by the name Savy James."

Will chuckled. Wrapping his fingers around the base of Tricksy's neck, he gave a tug. Will met Tricksy's lips with a slight brush of his.

"The thing about bullies is that they can only be if they have a victim."

Tricksy jerked her head out of Will's hold. "Are you saying I'm a victim?"

"No. No, that's not what I'm saying." Will reached for her hands. When he got hold of her, his hold was gentle, but absolute. There was no way he was letting her go now that he had her. "I'm saying you need to use your words."

"I tried that tonight. Didn't you catch the performance on the stage? She stole my spotlight. Like always."

"Not with that first song," said Will. "In that performance, you were brilliant."

Tricksy squeezed his hands, leaning across the middle console. "I didn't want to sing the second song."

"I know." Will squeezed back.

When Tricksy had sung that song back in the dive bar last week, her voice had been resonant. But tonight, it had been resigned and reedy. Her performance confirmed for him more than words ever could that she was finally over his brother.

It was his cue that she was ready to move forward. Which meant that it was the perfect time to come clean about his involvement in her past. The book in his back pocket was burning a hole in his jeans, eager to finally come into the spotlight.

"Tricksy... there's something I've been meaning to tell you. It's about our past."

"I don't want to revisit the past, Will. I want to talk about a future. Our future. Because I realized tonight that I want a future with you."

It was Tricksy that cupped Will's cheek in her hand. She brushed her lips against his. Softly, carefully. Will held still, letting her sample him. Tricksy was worthy of savoring every taste, every morsel.

"I realize that I deserve to be happy," she said, her mouth still pressed against his.

"You do." Will wobbled at her lower lip.

"I was worried about being happy and how it might affect my singing. Isn't that crazy?"

"Insane." Will moved his attentions to Tricksy's top lip.

"But tonight when I was on that stage, and looking at you, I hit notes I didn't even know I could."

Will pulled away, but only far enough that a breath could get between them. He stared into Tricksy's gaze and his heart banged against his chest in double time rhythm.

"It is insane," Tricksy said. "It's insane that I should feel this way about you so quick. But somehow I think this feeling has always been here inside of me. Even after all these years, I feel like we've never been apart. I feel like you've always been there, in my life, somewhere up high, watching over me."

Will opened his mouth to tell her that he had, that he'd always made a point to seek her out wherever she was performing. Though he doubted that would sound as romantic in his head as it would out loud. Besides, he still had to get to the part about him putting words in Topher's mouth.

"Tricks, I know you don't want to talk about the past." Will looked down at their joined hands. One day, he wanted to put a ring on her finger. "But there's something I need to get off my chest in order for us to move forward."

"Topher?"

"Yes, about Topher."

"Topher?"

Something in her tone made him look up. She wasn't looking at him. She was looking out the driver's side window. Her expression was one of wary incredulity.

A dark figure stood outside the car door. A dark figure with a square jaw and blond locks that had grown longer than Air Force regulation.

"Topher?" Will said.

Topher bent down. He tapped at the window and then made a motion for Will to roll it down.

"Hey, bro. Hey, Tricks."

"Topher?" both Will and Tricksy repeated.

"Sorry to interrupt the make-out session, but the front door is locked and I don't have my keys."

"Topher?" Tricksy said again, her voice losing its surprise and growing angry. "What are you doing here?"

"I live here. And I hear there's going to be two weddings. By the looks of you two, I'm guessing that's increased to three."

"You think Will and I are going to get married?" said Tricksy.

"That's what it looks like to me," said Topher. He turned his gaze from Tricksy to Will. "Looks like you told her everything, and it's fine."

"Everything?" asked Tricksy. "What everything?"

"You know; how he's the one that fed me those lines about adoring me amour back when we were kids-"

"It was the dear that I adore," said Will with a huff at his words being butchered even more. "Devoted to mon amour."

"Yup, that. What he said. The words that made

you fall for me. Now you see that it was him you were really in love with and not me. I told you I wasn't the guy you thought I was. Now, you believe me."

CHAPTER TWENTY

"**W**ill? What's he talking about?"

It was surprisingly easy to tear her gaze away from Topher. Tricksy had once believed his face to be so interesting. But today it looked tired. There were lines and dark circles under Topher's eyes. The indents of mischief that had always stretched at the corners of his eyes looked like they'd been carrying something heavy. The angles at the edges of his mouth weighed down as though he'd been frowning a lot recently.

In another life, Tricksy would've gone to Topher. She would've urged him to unburden himself in hopes it would draw them closer together. Right now, she didn't care a wit about what was bothering him.

Her gaze went to Will. Will didn't look much better than his brother did. The smooth planes of his forehead now creased with a burden that looked as heavy as Topher's. Will's soft lips that had kissed her silly a moment ago were pursed, as though he were holding back words. He hadn't been able to take his eyes off her all night, but now his attention was fixed on Will.

"Will?" she tried again. "Will, what's he talking about?"

The moment the words left her mouth, her own lips pursed. Will turned to her, and the look in his eyes made her heart thud. She had no clue what Topher meant about telling her everything. The way worry settling into the grooves of Will's brow told her it might be best if she were left in the dark.

But that wasn't the relationship she had with Will. They didn't have secrets. There were no lies between them.

"Tricks." Will reached for her, but she shrugged from his touch.

Her rejection shocked him as much as her. It was Will's touch she craved more than anything. Definitely more than Topher's. But she also wanted to be in Will's embrace more than she wanted her sister's hug.

Tricksy knew that whatever Will had to say, she didn't want to hear it. She knew it would unravel the beautifully woven fairytale she'd thread around their love story. The threads were all about to come apart. Then she'd be left standing alone, just like with her sisters.

And all because of Topher.

She glared at him as he stood outside the driver's side door. Tricksy reached for the passenger door handle, jerking the car door open and slamming it with all her might. She rounded on Topher, her index finger pointing at him accusingly.

"Why can't you just let me be happy?" she shouted at him.

"Me?" Topher pointed his thumb at his chest.

There had been a time that Tricksy had reveled in being wrapped up in his arms. Topher hadn't offered her many hugs. He wasn't the touchy feely type. Not unless there was making out involved. His hugs had never been about making her feel better. They had always been about him, about his wants, about his needs.

Tricksy took a step back from him. She didn't want to give anything away. She barely had anything left for herself. She just wanted someone to hold her, to comfort her.

Will climbed out of the driver's seat, his arms outstretched to her. More than anything, Tricksy wanted to go into his arms. She knew that everything she was missing could be found there.

"It's not his fault," said Will. "It's mine."

Those words called Tricksy up short. Will was meant to be on her side. So why was he standing in support of Topher?

Oh, right? Because there was something she hadn't been told? Something that would prove Topher wasn't the man she thought he was. Tricksy didn't need anyone to tell her that… anymore.

She'd figured it out on her own. Sure, it had taken years. But she'd learned her lesson.

"It was me," said Will.

That was something Tricksy now knew for sure. It was Will. It was Will she wanted to be with. It was Will that she was truly falling in love with.

"When we were kids and Topher was wooing you. It was me."

"I don't know what that even means?"

Will came to her, taking her hands in his. "I told him what to say to get him to go out with you. I feed him the lines."

Tricksy looked down at the hands that were always sure. She looked at the shoulder that had never let her down. She looked in to the eyes of the man she trusted above all others. "You... what?"

"Because it was what I felt for you." Will's hold tightened on her hands, as though he was frightened she'd try to get away. "I gave him all my feelings for you because you wanted romance in a package that was him."

Tricksy's head was hurting. Probably because it had begun playing a tennis match between the brothers. She looked at Will, then at Topher. Then back to Will, and once more at Topher.

It had always been Topher who had said one thing and did another. Now she saw that it was Will that did nothing while telling Topher what to say. Which was worse?

Finally, her gaze settled on Will. "You lied to me."

"I... yes. Yes, I did."

Will let go of her hands. He hung his head. All the fight gone out of him.

Tricksy turned on her heel to storm away. The sound of her stems impacting the ground was the loudest thing in the night. What she did not hear, what surprised her most, was that she didn't hear Will coming behind her.

CHAPTER TWENTY-ONE

"What are you doing here, Topher?" Will didn't take his eyes off of Tricksy as she walked away from him. Every fiber of his being told him to run after her, to whirl her around and make her understand. He hadn't done what he'd done to hurt her. He had just wanted to make her happy.

"Why does everyone keep asking me that?" Topher moved into Will's line of vision, but Will looked right through the man. "I do live here, you know. Technically, at least. It's my permanent address."

Will glanced at his brother. That one glance caused concern where Will didn't want to care. He tried not to see the bags under Topher's eyes. He tried to ignore the wariness in the frown lines. He tried to shrug off the tension he saw in his brother's shoulders.

The sound of the door to the guesthouse slamming shut broke the spell Tricksy had over Will and his full attention snapped to Topher.

"You're in trouble?" said Will.

Topher bit at his lower lip before opening his mouth to respond. Whatever came out of his mouth, Will knew to disregard. That lip bite was his tell. He was about to lie.

"I'm good, as always." Topher gave a shrug and looked towards the house.

That was his other tell. Whenever he lied, he always looked around to see if their father was nearby. Topher might mislead his brothers, but he would never lie to Father Matthews. It was late enough for their father to be in bed.

With the coast clear, Topher turned back to Will. "It's not me who's in trouble. I thought you told her?"

"I was about to," said Will. His nostrils flared at the words. When he inhaled, he caught the distinct smell of a woman's perfume on his brother's shirt. Here Will was about to lose the only woman he ever loved, and Topher had already picked up, and likely discarded, the next woman waiting in line for his attentions.

"I was about to tell her," Will said, casting a glance at the guest house, wishing Tricksy could hear him. "I had to make sure she was over you. And she is. She's over you."

Topher made a dismissive sound. "No woman is ever over me."

Will whirled back to his brother. His fists were clenched in anger. His exhale was loud and harsh as it passed his lips. The air was forceful enough to make Topher wince.

"This is not my fault," said Topher.

"Nothing is ever your fault, because you never take responsibility. Only credit."

In the distance, Will heard the sound of tires on gravel. Car doors opened and shut. He made out the soft murmurs of his brothers and their fiancées coming towards them.

"It's not like I want her." Topher waved a dismissive hand towards the guest house. "She was fun for a while. But you can go and have her."

"Go and have her?" Will took another deep breath. This one came out just as harsh as the rest of them. He was having trouble using his words because his teeth were grinding against each other so hard. "She's not a piece of candy we're sharing."

"No?" Topher flashed his wicked grin. "It seems like you were having a treat when I walked up on you making out just now."

Will rolled his eyes at his brother. His fists clenched harder. Topher could be callous. It was why Will had felt the need to feed him lines for Tricksy. He'd wanted her to have the romance and poetry she deserved. Now he saw exactly why she'd written that angsty breakup song. Topher did have a habit of mishandling things so that they broke, and the pieces never fit together quite right again.

"Sorry if I didn't realize how serious you were," Topher was saying. "I thought you'd just fulfill your boyish fantasies with a kiss or something and move on. Tricks is a handful."

There were no more words left in his throat. It closed up. As did his fists. But it was his fists that had something to say.

Will's fist lashed out before he could stop it. Topher went down to one knee, his hand covering his nose. Red oozed from between his fingers.

"Boys!"

Up on the porch, Father Matthews stood peering down at them. It was rare that the old man raised his voice in anger at his sons. The strain on his father's face had Will's hands instantly unclenched. The last thing he wanted to do was cause his father any stress or harm.

Will looked down at his father's side to see Ash. The kid's eyes were wide as he took in the scene. It was then that Will knew he'd caused more harm than he meant, and to more people than he wanted to hurt.

Charlie and Joe dashed between their brothers. Joe crouched down to Topher, one hand keeping him down, the other checking out the bleeder. Charlie made himself a roadblock in front of Will.

It was unnecessary. With that punch, all the anger had exploded out of Will. There was nothing left inside of him.

"Walk it off," Charlie said to Will.

Will did just that. He turned on his heel and headed into the woods. He walked until the red of his anger had dimmed and the darkness of night claimed him whole.

CHAPTER TWENTY-TWO

ricksy flopped herself down on the sofa in the guest house. She stared at nothing in the silence. The silence grew so loud she couldn't bear it.

There wasn't a television set in the place. The Matthews had never been fans of that style of entertainment. They'd always insisted there was too much to do outside on a working ranch than to sit on one's backside and watch others do their business.

Tricksy switched on the old-fashioned radio on the counter. Every station played a love song. An old somebody-done-somebody-else-wrong love song. A new somebody-done-somebody-else-wrong love song. And even one I-love-me-some-him love song.

After hearing that last one, she didn't change the station. She switched the device off and flopped back down on the couch, resuming staring at nothing in the silence. That's how her sister found her.

"I suppose this is somehow my fault, too," said Savy.

Savy stood in the door of the guest house. The moon cast her sister in an otherworldly glow. Tricksy looked up at her sister... and promptly burst into tears.

"Tricks, honey?"

The door slammed shut. The moon's light faded. Arms came around her and squeezed her tight.

"Baby girl, what's wrong?"

Tricksy hugged Savy back so tightly, so fiercely, that Savy tumbled down onto the couch beside her. Without wasting any time, Tricksy crawled into her sister's arms, practically climbing into Savy's lap. Savy didn't utter a sound of protest. She wrapped her arms around her sister like she was a baby and began to rock.

By the time Tricksy realized she had cried her eyes out, she opened her eyes to see that she was surrounded by Savy on one side and Foxy on the other.

Savy had one arm wrapped around Tricksy, while the other held her hand. Foxy gripped Tricksy's other hand tightly in hers. It had been so long since her sisters had both stood by her side. A few more tears trickled down her cheeks before she could get herself together and come to sit on the sofa cushions between them.

"It's Topher, isn't it?" said Savy. "I saw him outside. Is that why Will gave him that shiner?"

"Shiner?" asked Tricksy.

"What did he say to you?" asked Foxy. "Did he try to win you back?"

Tricksy wanted to laugh at that. But she was still too tear-logged. Her humor had no purchase from which to launch even a small giggle.

Instead of laughing, she asked, "Will broke Topher's nose?"

"That he did," said Savy. "And all I have to say is *finally.*"

"Will's not a fighter," Tricksy insisted.

Tricksy had known Will Matthews for more than half her life. Nothing rattled the man. Not to anger, and not to passion.

Well, she'd have to strike the passion part. He'd shown her more passion in the last couple of days than any song she'd ever sung.

"He wouldn't have broken Topher's nose unless he made a pass at you," said Foxy.

"Did Topher make a pass at you?" asked Savy. "If he did, I'll bust his lip to match his crooked nose."

"Topher didn't make a pass at me," said Tricksy. "He implied Will was keeping something from me."

"What could Will possibly have to keep from you?" asked Savy.

Tricksy hated to admit it. More to herself than to her sisters. "It was Will that wrote those poems for me all those years ago, not Topher."

"So, Topher lied and said they were his?" said Savy. "The jerk."

Tricksy shook her head. "I think Will put him up to it."

"Why would Will do that?" said Savy.

"Because..." Tricksy sniffled at the realization. "Because Will knew I wanted Topher, and he wanted me to be happy, even if it wasn't with him."

"I'm not following you, sweetie." Savy shook her head, but she didn't let go of Tricksy's hand.

"I am," said Foxy, as she squeezed Tricksy's other hand. "Will has always been in love with you. But you've always had a crush on Topher. Will didn't think he could compete and so he tried to give you what he thought you wanted. That's his way."

"I mean," Savy began, "it does make sense that Will would've written those words than it does Topher."

It did make sense. But it didn't make it right.

"But he shouldn't have Cyrano de Bergerac'd you," said Savy. "That was wrong. They were both wrong. I'm gonna go give them both matching bloody noses."

Tricksy yanked her older sister back down onto the couch. Savy came with a begrudging grin. She wrapped her arms around Tricksy and bussed a kiss to her temple.

"Fine," said Savy. "You fight your own battles. We'll be standing by for backup if you need us."

That particular fight with the men in her love life would have to wait. Tricksy was far too preoccupied, and too happy, with being in the spotlight of her sisters' attentions.

CHAPTER TWENTY-THREE

ill's fist smarted where the skin tore after the impact with his brother's face. Topher had a hard head, so no wonder Will was in pain. But he wasn't the only one in pain.

From his place in the woods, he could see glimpses of his family. Charlie made angry gestures at Topher. Joe stood between them, making calming movements. Their father stood over his sons watching the boys with what Will knew was dismay.

A handful of words. One action and everyone he cared about had gotten hurt. This was why he didn't fight back. It did no good.

Tricksy felt betrayed. Topher was bleeding. And Will had no one to blame but himself.

He'd finally had the opportunity to use his own

words himself and he had stalled. From his back pocket, he fished out the proof copy of the book of poetry he'd authored. In the dark, he couldn't see a single phrase. What good were his words now?

"Wow, what a punch! I thought you said you didn't know any martial arts."

Will sighed. He didn't need the moon's light to let him know that Ash had followed him into the woods.

"You gotta teach me how to hit like that. If I get in one good shot, those bullies will never mess with me again."

"That's not a bully, Ash. That's my brother."

Topher was the brother that had bullied Will the worst when he'd first come to the foster home. Topher was also the brother that had protected Will fiercely after they were finally able to communicate with each other. Tonight, Will had hurt his brother for simply speaking the truth.

A harsh truth. An inconvenient truth, but a truth no less. Tricksy was a handful. But she was a handful that Will wanted to hold on to for the rest of his life.

Will had had boyish fantasies about her for most of his life. But he was a grown man now. Not a child. He was purposeful with his words as well as his deeds. What was between him and Tricksy was real, and he wasn't giving up on it. It was worth fighting for.

"You gonna go finish him off?" Ash's gaze was down, focused on Will's hand.

Looking down at his hands, Will saw that he was flexing his fists. "No, Ash. Violence is never the answer."

"Yeah, but you look like you're ready to fight."

"I am ready to fight." Will marched back towards the house. Behind him he heard Ash mutter "Cool" and fall into step with him.

As Will neared the house, his father was the first to see him. Father Matthews's gaze narrowed on Will. But something in Will's expression told his father that there was no cause for alarm. He gave a nod that was as much of a blessing.

Will's heart filled with gratitude at the motion. His father knew that he wasn't a violent man. Even if his two eldest brothers moved in front of Topher as though they were his bodyguards. Will very nearly lost the battle with rolling his eyes.

"I walked it off," Will said, holding out his hand to Topher.

Topher looked down at Will's hand, then back at Will. He shouldered his way between Charlie and Joe to come to stand before Will. Topher took Will's hand -Will's injured hand- with his own and squeezed; hard.

Will winced.

Topher smirked.

"I love her," Will said.

"I know," said Topher.

Now it was Will who squeezed his brother's hand, hard enough for Topher to wince. "You disrespect her again, and we'll be right back here."

"Fair enough." Topher didn't quite hide the wince of pain at Will's grip. "That's some right hook you got there for a pacifist."

"She's worth fighting for," said Will.

"Then you better go to her." Topher released Will's hand and gave him a pat on the back. Though the pat was much more like a slap.

In his typical fashion, Will let that slide. Topher was an Alpha dog. Will had no issues running near the back of the pack. He had nothing to prove. Not when he was very close to having everything he could ever want in this life.

Will turned to find Ash studying the scene from the side of the porch. There was equal disappointment, as there was curiosity, on the kid's face. Will knew if this kid was to make it in this world, he would need the balance of those scales tipped a bit.

"You saw what just happened there?" said Will.

"Yeah," said Ash.

"You saw that the fighting didn't solve anything?"

"I don't know, Mr. Will? I think the big guy won't mess with you again."

"If I hadn't calmed down and come back and talked it over, it would've hurt my whole family. Fighting with fists never solves anything."

"Unless the other guy hits you first," said Topher.

"Excuse me." Will faced his brother. "Do we need to repeat the lesson we just learned again?"

"Nope," Topher grinned as the blood trickled down his nose. He peered down at Ash. "Use your words first. Fists second, but only if the other guy raises his first. Then you hit him hard enough so that he stays down."

Topher ducked into the house behind their father before Will could give any kind of response, verbal or physical.

"It's good to be home," Topher said as the screen door closed behind him.

Father Matthews let out a long sigh. Joe gave a shrug as if to say *What do you expect from a Matthews.*

Charlie came up and clapped Ash on the back. "I'll take over the after school special lesson from here. Will, you need to go sort things out with Tricksy."

Will did have to do that. But how? It was words that had gotten him into trouble. How could he use his words to get him out of it?

CHAPTER TWENTY-FOUR

*T*ricksy was certain she'd woken the rooster up with all her moving about. But even long after the bird had made his cries, she still hadn't seen Will all morning.

Had he left? That was his way. Will Matthews avoided confrontations at all costs. Though one look at Topher's black eye and swollen nose told her differently.

"Ouch," she said, as Topher came out of the barn.

His eye was a light shade of blue mixed with a hint of purple. There was redness all around his nose. But instead of making him look a fright, it made him look like a rogue.

Of course it did. He was Topher.

"You should see the other guy," he said.

Tricksy's back went straight and tension radiated out to her fingertips, pulling them into fists. "You hit Will!"

"I didn't touch him." Topher put up his hands to ward off another impending attack. He jerked a thumb at his swollen face. "He did this for you."

"For me?" All the tension left Tricksy's body on a sigh. It was crazy that the thought of her sweet-tempered Will would do this kind of damage for her. Then she had to wonder… "Why? What did you do to make him act out?"

Topher shrugged, then winced at the movement. "I may have made an inappropriate comment."

"About me?"

"Look, I'm sorry, Tricks. For the comment, but also for how it went down between us all those years ago."

Tricksy gave her head a wobble. Was the mighty Christopher Matthews actually apologizing? Tricksy realized how much she'd needed to hear those words.

But what she wanted more was to talk to Will. To hear his words.

"He's in love with you, you know."

So everyone kept saying to her, including Will.

"Then why didn't he just tell me that himself? Why did he give you his words?"

"Because you didn't feel the same way about him, and he wanted you to have what you wanted. So, he told me what to say to make you happy."

The anger and hurt that had grown inside Tricksy's gut last night evaporated in one instance. It was true that Will had mislead her. But the reason that he mislead her is what gutted her.

"I don't think he thought he deserved you. At least not back then. He knew you had a thing for me. Because, of course, what woman wouldn't -Ouch!"

Tricksy punched Topher in the shoulder. He was lucky it had been in the fleshy part of his arm and not in his face. She was sorely tempted, but despite the twinkle of mischief in his eyes, she saw something there she'd never seen before; sorrow.

What else did Topher Matthews have to be sorry about? No sooner had she spied it than he shuttered his gaze and turned away from her.

"Where is he?" she asked.

Topher pointed to the barn. "Helping Joe and Charlie with their vows."

Tricksy moved past Topher, finally leaving what she thought they had behind her, and headed into the barn. Inside, Will had his back to the door. He leaned against a wall with his brothers facing him. Joe and Charlie had their heads buried in a small book.

"These are good, bro," Charlie was saying. "Can I use this one for my vows to Savy?"

"Oh, that line would be good for Foxy," said Joe.

"No." Will snatched the book from them. "I wrote these for Tricksy. I'm not letting anyone have those words from my heart about her again. I have, in fact, learned my lesson."

"Yeah?" said Charlie. His gaze had lifted and was fixed on Tricksy. "So, which of these poems are you going to use when you make your vows to her?"

"I've gotta win her back first," said Will.

"Just pretend," said Joe. His gaze also had found Tricksy standing in the doorway. "If you were down on one knee right now, what would you say to her?"

"There are too many words I want to say to her," said Will. "That's why I wrote them all down in this book of poetry. It's everything I couldn't say to her myself."

"You wrote me a book of poetry?"

Will whipped around to see her. His eyes went wide at the sight of her, as though she was the sun and he was soaking it all in on a cold day.

Tricksy walked closer to him. Joe and Charlie

made their way past her and out of the barn. Once Tricksy was standing before Will, the two of them simply stood still and silent, gazing at one another as though seeing them anew.

"Tricks… I was going to come find you. To tell you everything. I had planned to tell you everything soon. I've been a coward about love."

"Tell that to Topher's nose."

Will let out a harsh laugh and then promptly winced. "You know that's not me. But I will fight for you. I'm going to fight to win you back. I'm going to sweep you so far off your feet you'll-"

Tricksy snatched the book from his hand. She gave him her back as she turned the pages. Inside the book was verse upon verse of the most tear-jerking and heartfelt rhymes she'd ever read.

"You say you'll do anything to win me back?"

"Yes," Will said. "Name it."

Tricksy held up the book of poems. "I want these. I want to use your words. I want to sing them."

Will's smile was slow, but as it spread, it lit up his face. "They're yours. Every last one of them."

"I'm going to give you credit this time," she said.

"All I'll ask is that you take my name."

Will wrapped his arms around her. Tricksy came into his embrace. She bypassed the inclination to rest her head on his shoulder. Instead, she went right for what she truly wanted. Her hand rested at his heart as she aimed for his lips.

Will met her kiss with the kind of passion that songs and poems were written about. In fact, once the kissing was done, the poet and songstress got down to just that. They composed a bevy of rhymes that were sure to make all who listened get up on their feet and sway to the rhythm of love.

opher scratched at his chest. The raised bumps he found there irritated him more than the fading bruise below his eye did. He'd had his nose broken many a time in his life. At times because he opened his mouth. At other times because his gaze had strayed to a woman who wasn't as free as her flirtatious gaze let on. But mostly he'd gotten his nose broken in the heat of battle.

Topher had been a fighter all his life. Even before joining the armed forces. He loved as hard as he fought.

Though love was a strong word. The raised skin over his heart agreed with him. He peered in the mirror at the angry scar. Thinking about how it got there had his heart skipping a beat.

"You all right there, son?"

Topher snatched the edges of his shirt together, fastening the buttons with quick fingers as he met his father's gaze. He hadn't meant to leave the bedroom door open. He'd only come in to grab a change of shirt after the day's chores.

Things were busier than usual on the ranch after the weddings. Both Charlie and Savy and Joe and Foxy were away on their honeymoons. By the time the two couples came back, there would be three prefabricated homes on the ranch. Three because Will had wasted no time in proposing to Tricksy, and that wedding would be happening at the end of the month. Joe and his dad were still hearing it from the Silver sisters that they weren't building the homes themselves as their father, the dearly departed General Silver, had had them do when they were just girls.

But the adults on the Flying Cross Ranch didn't have time to build new homes, along with fostering five kids, and managing a working ranch. Topher was home on borrowed time. He only had a few months left before he signed a new enlistment contract. He just had to take care of a few things before he went back into the Air Force.

"Dad..." he began and stopped. Topher had never

been good at asking for help. He preferred to do everything on his own. Being a burden was what had gotten him thrown into foster care at a young age. He'd vowed never to be too much of a handful to his adoptive parents, not after everything they'd done for him. But this request wasn't for him. Not exactly.

"Dad," he began again.

"What is it, son?" Father Matthews came into the room, shutting the door behind him. It was as though his father knew he needed privacy to make this request.

"I know we're a bit crowded here on the ranch, but I was wondering if we could make space for one more?"

His father's face was a mask of patience as he regarded his son. Haran Matthews had to know instinctively that there was more to this story than Topher was letting on.

"Since the guest house will be empty, I wanted to let a buddy of mine use it while they recover from their injuries."

The scar on Topher's chest itched again, but he stopped himself from scratching at it. Still, his father's eyes went to that very spot, as though it called to him.

"A Wounded Warrior?" asked Father Matthews.

"Yes, Airman Toni Solis."

"Of course, son. Any friend of yours, and any fellow airman, is welcome here." His father gave a nod and headed for the door. "Just let me know when he'll arrive."

Topher gulped, trying to hold down the half truth he'd just let slip by. The whole truth was that Airman Antonia Solis wasn't a man. Even more of the truth was that it was Topher's fault that she had been injured in the first place. At least now he had the chance to make it up to her by bringing her here to the ranch to get better.

Are you the kind of reader that loves it when a bad boy falls hard for the right girl? Then you don't want to miss the epic downfall of Topher Matthews in
"His Vow to Trust"
Book Four in the Flying Cross Ranch Romances!

Shanae Johnson was raised by Saturday Morning cartoons and After School Specials. She still doesn't understand why there isn't a life lesson that ties the issues of the day together just before bedtime. While she's still waiting for the meaning of it all, she writes stories to try and figure it all out. Her books are wholesome and sweet, but her are heroes are hot and heroines are full of sass!

And by the way, the E elongates the A. So it's pronounced Shan-aaaaaaaa. Perfect for a hero to call out across the moors, or up to a balcony, or to blare outside her window on a boombox. If you hear him calling her name, please send him her way!

You can sign up for Shanae's Reader Group and receive a FREE NOVELLA in this world at

https://shanaejohnson.com/ReaderGroup

ALSO BY SHANAE JOHNSON

a Flying Cross Ranch Romance

His Vow to Love

His Vow to Treasure

His Vow to Adore

His Vow to Trust

His Vow to Respect

His Vow to Defend

The Silver Star Ranch Romances

His Pledge to Honor

His Pledge to Cherish

His Pledge to Protect

His Pledge to Obey

His Pledge to Have

His Pledge to Hold

The Brides of Purple Heart

On His Bended Knee

Hand Over His Heart

Offering His Arm

His Permanent Scar

Having His Back

In Over His Head

Always On His Mind

Every Step He Takes

In His Good Hands

www.ingramcontent.com/pod-product-compliance
Lightning Source LLC
Chambersburg PA
CBHW060921140726
47996CB00001B/331